CONTENTS

06	I OWN THIS
08	3 IN A ROW
09	CHAMPIONSHIP CHALLENGE
10	CROWD CONTROL
11	PROFILE: RASMUS HØJLUND
12	COULDA, WOULDA... SHOULDA?
14	SPOT THE BALL
16	RULES OF THE GAME
18	MATCH OF THE CENTURY
20	INTERVIEW: LEWIS MILEY
22	SPOT THE BOSS
24	SHOOT'S FOOTBALL A TO Z QUIZ
26	PL NEW KIDS ON THE BLOCK
28	INTERVIEW: AGGIE BEEVER-JONES
30	SUPER TALL!
31	SUPER FAST!
32	PL RECORD BREAKERS
34	BADGE MASH-UP!
35	BADGE TRUE OR FALSE?
36	INTERVIEW: KOBBIE MAINOO
38	SUPERSTAR SUPERCAR
39	PROFILE: LEWIS DUNK
40	WSL NEW KIDS ON THE BLOCK
42	INTERVIEW: BETH MEAD
44	WHO IS THE GOAT?
46	SHOOT FOOTY QUIZ
48	BEST & WORST KITS... EVER!
50	INTERVIEW: MORGAN ROGERS
52	INTERVIEW: CONOR BRADLEY
54	SPOT THE DIFFERENCE
55	PROFILE: LEON BAILEY
56	SCANDINAVIAN DREAM TEAM
58	2024 WINNERS
60	PHIL FODEN TROPHY HUNTER
62	BARCLAYS WOMEN'S SUPER LEAGUE
64	PLAYERS AND THEIR PETS
65	ANIMAL SPOTTING
66	DECLAN RICE 10 FACTS
67	PROFILE: MICKY VAN DE VEN
68	DID YOU KNOW?
70	INTERVIEW: COLE PALMER
72	SILLY SHADOWS
73	TRANSFER CHALLENGE
74	JUDE BELLINGHAM
76	ANSWERS

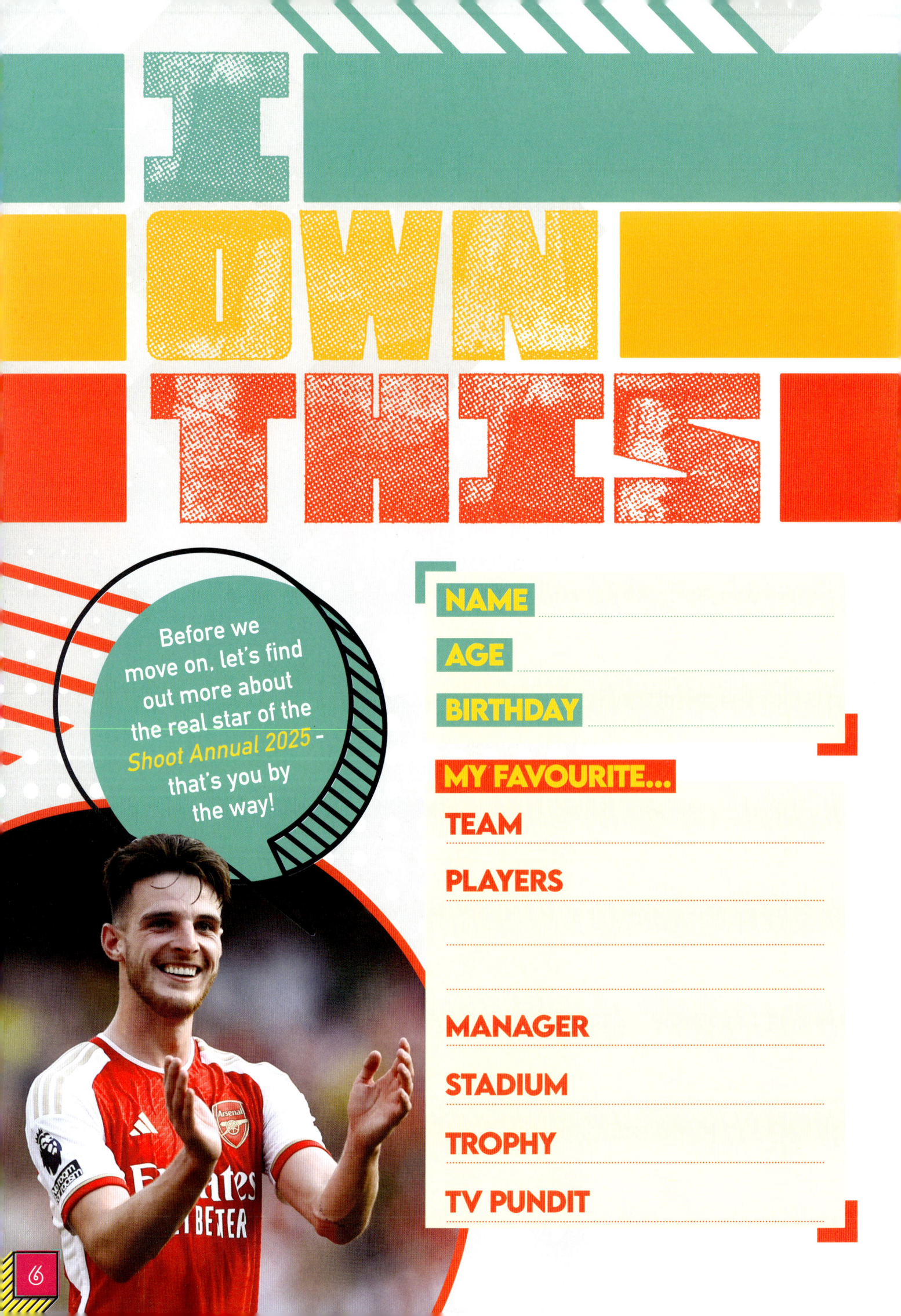

I OWN THIS

Before we move on, let's find out more about the real star of the *Shoot Annual 2025* - that's you by the way!

NAME ....
AGE ....
BIRTHDAY ....

MY FAVOURITE...

TEAM ....
PLAYERS ....
....
....
MANAGER ....
STADIUM ....
TROPHY ....
TV PUNDIT ....

ABOUT ME...

THE TEAM I PLAY FOR

THE COLOUR OF OUR KIT

THE POSITION I PLAY

THE NUMBER ON MY SHIRT

MY FAVOURITE TEAMMATE

THE COLOUR OF MY BOOTS

RIGHT OR LEFT FOOTED

Here's your chance to rate yourself. Colour in the stars you think match your skill level.

PLAYER RATING

PACE ★★★★★★★★★★★★★★★★★★★★
SHOOTING ★★★★★★★★★★★★★★★★★★★★
PASSING ★★★★★★★★★★★★★★★★★★★★
DRIBBLING ★★★★★★★★★★★★★★★★★★★★
DEFENDING ★★★★★★★★★★★★★★★★★★★★
STRENGTH ★★★★★★★★★★★★★★★★★★★★

3 IN A ROW

10 players, 10 squad numbers and 10 clubs – get yourself some different coloured pens and join each player to the correct club and number!

PHIL FODEN

JARROD BOWEN

BETH MEAD

ALEXIS MAC ALLISTER

ALEX IWOBI

8 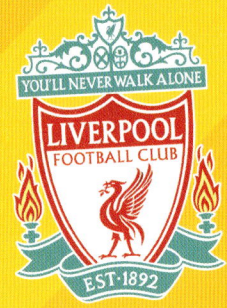 37  20

 20 10  14

   11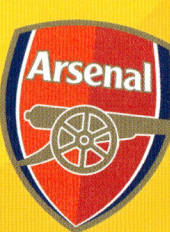

9  22   47

MICKY VAN DE VEN

SAM KERR

OLLIE WATKINS

BRUNO FERNANDES

ALEXANDER ISAK

ANSWERS ON PAGES 76-77

CHAMPIONSHIP CHALLENGE

One of the toughest leagues to get out of – the Championship! How good is your knowledge of English football's second division? There are 12 Championship clubs in our wordsearch, see how many you can find!

B	H	N	G	E	I	C	P	N	D	C	Z	H	N	I	A	Y	B
L	G	U	G	G	F	Y	A	F	O	P	G	S	R	G	R	T	L
R	U	T	L	J	T	U	U	V	Q	U	B	X	S	L	V	I	A
D	N	V	Z	L	O	F	E	U	O	T	J	X	T	E	Z	C	C
P	C	T	C	F	C	N	R	R	K	P	I	P	O	T	R	L	K
S	J	G	K	F	T	I	B	F	G	Q	A	Y	K	V	D	O	B
G	U	O	L	R	H	S	T	S	H	T	M	P	E	P	F	T	U
M	X	N	Y	K	E	R	E	Y	K	T	P	O	C	X	G	S	R
D	X	F	D	L	C	A	R	D	I	F	F	C	I	T	Y	I	N
Z	G	W	D	E	D	W	C	C	E	D	S	J	T	Q	F	R	R
Y	Q	D	Q	J	R	N	H	W	R	R	A	T	Y	P	D	B	O
Z	I	J	E	D	D	L	H	T	U	O	M	S	T	R	O	P	V
M	C	M	O	L	Q	D	A	K	H	F	A	X	X	K	T	A	E
R	N	Q	J	X	Z	D	Q	N	Y	T	Z	P	M	E	Y	K	R
E	R	U	S	T	O	A	N	F	D	A	T	J	E	S	M	K	S
N	Y	T	I	C	A	E	S	N	A	W	S	O	P	N	W	H	U
Q	S	Z	C	T	W	T	J	C	T	Q	Q	Q	Y	H	S	T	J
P	R	E	S	T	O	N	N	O	R	T	H	E	N	D	G	E	S

WATFORD **MIDDLESBROUGH** **CARDIFF CITY** **PORTSMOUTH**
BRISTOL CITY **PRESTON NORTH END** **COVENTRY** **HULL CITY**
STOKE CITY **SWANSEA CITY** **SUNDERLAND** **BLACKBURN ROVERS**

ANSWERS ON PAGES 76-77

CROWD CONTROL

Here's a real test of your Big Stadium knowledge! These stadiums have seen some epic games, but just how many fans got to see those games? Can you guess the capacity of each stadium? You have two options to choose from each time. Good luck!

OLD TRAFFORD — Manchester United
- 74,310 ☐
- 69,260 ☐

NOU CAMP — Barcelona
- 105,000 ☐
- 95,000 ☐

ANFIELD — Liverpool
- 61,015 ☐
- 55,700 ☐

PARC DES PRINCES — PSG
- 57,657 ☐
- 47,929 ☐

ALLIANZ ARENA — Bayern Munich
- 67,565 ☐
- 75,024 ☐

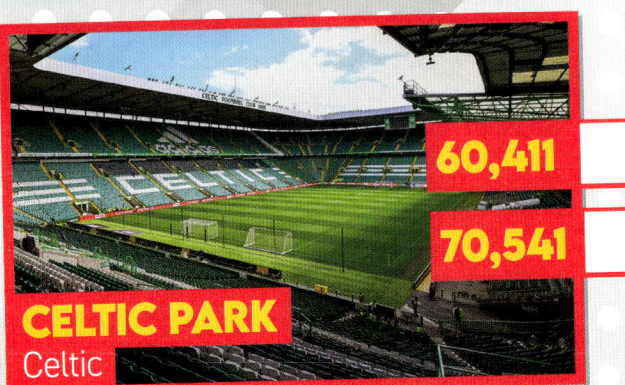
CELTIC PARK — Celtic
- 60,411 ☐
- 70,541 ☐

ST JAMES' PARK — Newcastle United
- 60,100 ☐
- 52,404 ☐

ANSWERS ON PAGES 76-77

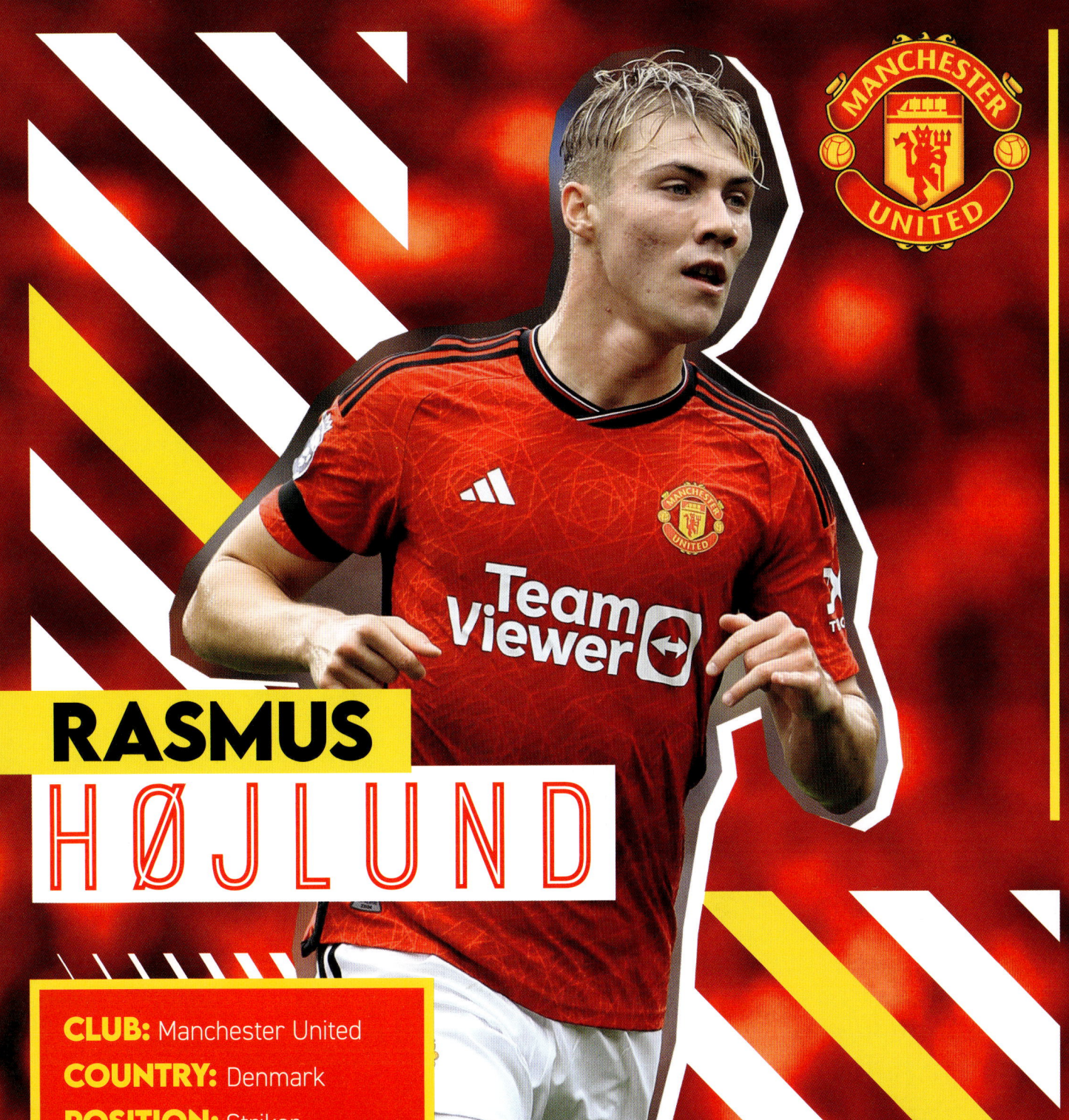

RASMUS HØJLUND

CLUB: Manchester United
COUNTRY: Denmark
POSITION: Striker
BORN: 4 February 2003
PREVIOUS CLUBS: FC Copenhagen, Sturm Graz, Atalanta

DID YOU KNOW?

Rasmus has two younger twin brothers – Oscar and Emil – who both play at the family home city club FC Copenhagen.

COULDA, WOULDA... SHOULDA?

Some players who have become legends for their country could have actually represented other nations if they had chosen to.

Players qualify to play for the country they were born in, the country they have lived in for a certain amount of time, or the country their parents or grandparents were born in.

Here is a selection of top players who you could have seen wearing the colours of a different country altogether.

If you could choose any player in the world to switch allegiance and play for your country, who would it be?

....

Alejandro GARNACHO

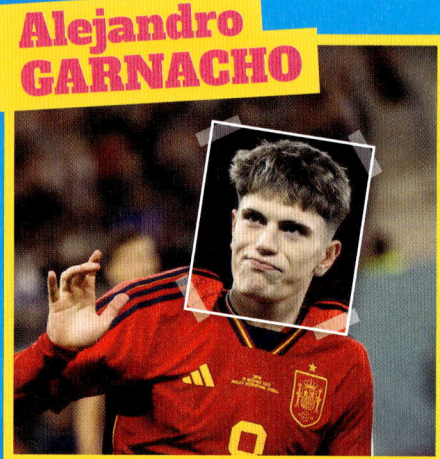

PLAYS FOR ARGENTINA
COULD HAVE PLAYED FOR SPAIN

Born in Madrid, the Manchester United winger actually played for Spain Under-18s before deciding to represent the nation his mother was born in — Argentina. Lucky for them!

Erling HAALAND

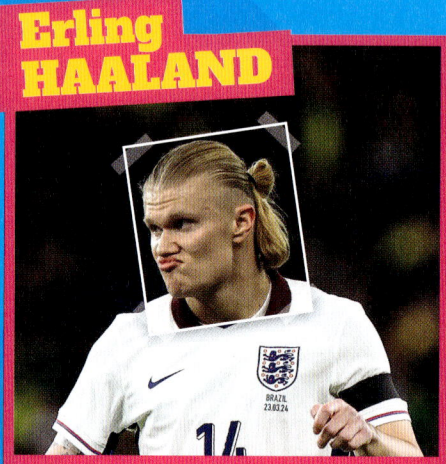

PLAYS FOR NORWAY
COULD HAVE PLAYED FOR ENGLAND

Yes, the world's most prolific goal-scorer was born in Yorkshire and could have played for England as his birth nation — but unluckily for the Three Lions, he chose his family's home country of Norway.

Scott McTOMINAY

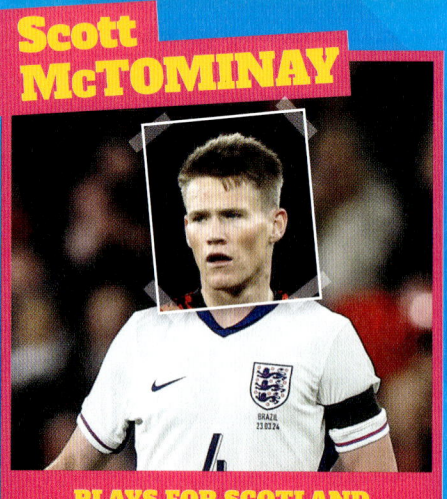

PLAYS FOR SCOTLAND
COULD HAVE PLAYED FOR ENGLAND

The Manchester United midfielder was born in Lancaster — he qualified to play for England but chose the country of his father's birth — Scotland — to play his international football.

Dejan KULUSEVSKI

PLAYS FOR SWEDEN
COULD HAVE PLAYED FOR NORTH MACEDONIA

Born in Stockholm, Sweden, his parents are Macedonian, and he represented their nation at youth level, but chose Sweden as a full international — a nation ranked about 40 places higher by FIFA.

Matheus NUNES

PLAYS FOR PORTUGAL
COULD HAVE PLAYED FOR BRAZIL

Manchester City's Matheus Nunes was born in Rio, but after living in Portugal for 10 years, chose to switch his allegiance to the Portuguese rather than play for Brazil.

Declan RICE

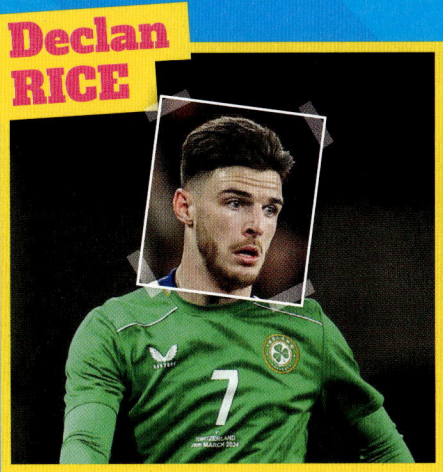

PLAYS FOR ENGLAND
COULD HAVE PLAYED FOR REPUBLIC OF IRELAND

Ireland's loss was very much England's gain! Although the Arsenal midfielder is English, he initially opted to play for the country of his grandparents and even played three matches for the greens!

Jack GREALISH

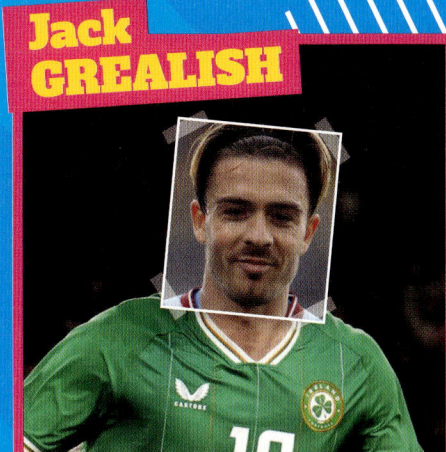

PLAYS FOR ENGLAND
COULD HAVE PLAYED FOR REPUBLIC OF IRELAND

'Super Jack' might be as Brummie as the Spaghetti Junction, but he represented Ireland through his grandparents at three different levels before switching to his birth nation 'England' in 2015.

Wilfried ZAHA

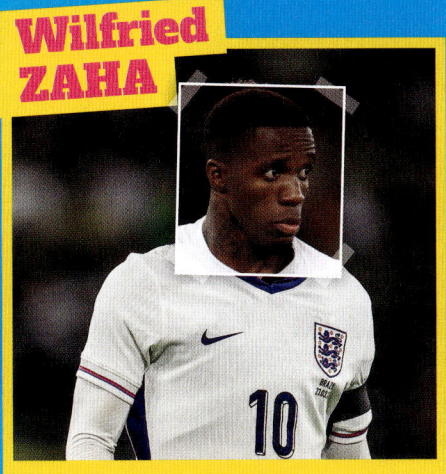

PLAYS FOR IVORY COAST
COULD HAVE PLAYED FOR ENGLAND

Zaha was born in Ivory Coast but became an English citizen after moving to London as a boy. He played in two international friendlies for England but in 2016, he switched to his birth nation Ivory Coast.

Kylian MBAPPE

PLAYS FOR FRANCE
COULD HAVE PLAYED FOR CAMEROON

One of the world's greatest forwards could have been competing in the Africa Cup of Nations. Born in Paris, his father was from Cameroon – though representing Les Bleus was never really in question!

Raheem STERLING

PLAYS FOR ENGLAND
COULD HAVE PLAYED FOR JAMAICA

He represented England with distinction, but the Chelsea forward was born in Jamaica and spent the early part of his life there. He could have played for the Reggae Boyz, but instead represented his adopted nation.

Lionel MESSI

PLAYS FOR ARGENTINA
COULD HAVE PLAYED FOR SPAIN

It's hard to imagine Messi playing for anyone other than Argentina, but he could have chosen La Roja. He lived in Barcelona from a young age and qualified for Spanish citizenship, plus his great grandfather was from Spain. But his heart was always Argentinian…

Fikayo TOMORI

PLAYS FOR ENGLAND
COULD HAVE PLAYED FOR CANADA OR NIGERIA

An interesting example of dual nationalities. The Milan defender, was born in Canada to Nigerian parents, so could have chosen to play for either nation! However, as a baby, his family moved to England and he became an English national – and chose the Three Lions!

SPOT THE BALL

Six balls have mysteriously appeared in each of these action shots below. Can you work out which is the real one?

GAME 1

ARSENAL V TOTTENHAM

GAME 2

BRIGHTON V ROMA

GAME 3
CHELSEA V MANCHESTER UNITED

GAME 4
ENGLAND V SWEDEN

ANSWERS ON PAGES 76-77

15

RULES OF THE GAME

Football has evolved over the years, with new rules, technology and regulations added along the way – but when did they actually come into play? Try and link the year with the ruling!

YELLOW AND RED CARDS

Players and team officials have been booked or sent off for many years, but yellow and red cards haven't always been around, in fact they weren't introduced until...

- 1970 ☐
- 1980 ☐
- 1990 ☐

VAR

VAR technology was used in various places around the world in a limited capacity for a number of years. VAR came to The Premier League at the start of the season in...

- 1999 ☐
- 2010 ☐
- 2019 ☐

GOAL-LINE TECHNOLOGY

One of the best innovations for football! Sensors around the goal-posts can detect whether the whole of the ball has crossed the goal-line or not – if even 1mm hasn't, it isn't a goal. Fans were happy when this rule came in to effect in...

- 2004 ☐
- 2014 ☐
- 2020 ☐

3 POINTS FOR A WIN

Believe it or not, teams only used to get two points for a win. But it was agreed that by making a win worth three points, teams were more likely to try and win the game which made football even more entertaining! This rule change happened in...

- 1971 ☐
- 1981 ☐
- 1991 ☐

EXTRA TIME

Test your rules and regulations knowledge with our true or false bonus quiz!

1 You cannot be offside from a throw-in.
TRUE ☐   FALSE ☐

2 The referee can be substituted for another referee.
TRUE ☐   FALSE ☐

3 If a team has five players sent off, the game is abandoned and replayed.
TRUE ☐   FALSE ☐

4 Teams must have a designated goalkeeper in order to play a match.
TRUE ☐   FALSE ☐

5 You can score a goal directly from a throw-in.
TRUE ☐   FALSE ☐

6 You can score a goal directly from a kick-off.
TRUE ☐   FALSE ☐

THE BACK-PASS RULE

Another positive rule change was when goalkeepers could no longer pick up a back pass from their own player, and instead would have to clear the ball with their feet. This was introduced to stop teams time-wasting. Sometimes, a goalkeeper will accidentally pick the ball up, resulting in a free-kick from inside the box, and this rule has been around since...

1990 ☐
1992 ☐
1995 ☐

PENALTY SHOOT-OUTS

There's nothing more dramatic than a penalty shoot-out! But this nail-biting way of deciding a match hasn't always been around. Love it, or hate it, 'pens' have only been a regular part of competitions since...

1970 ☐
1975 ☐
1980 ☐

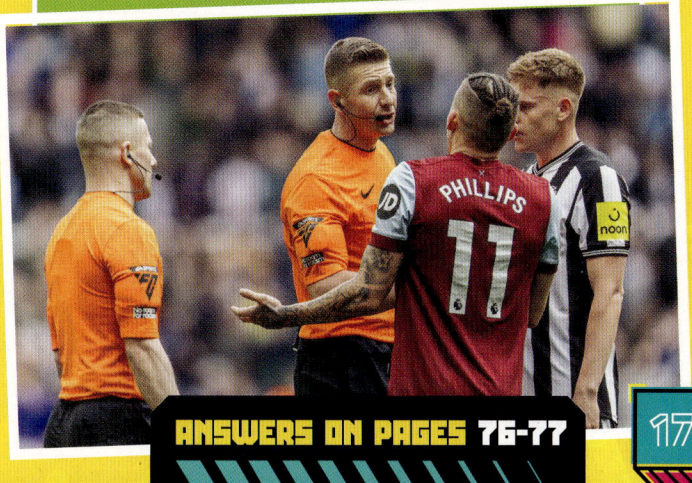

ANSWERS ON PAGES 76-77

MATCH OF THE CENTURY

Imagine you have been tasked with picking a World XI and a Premier League XI for a one-off game - who would make your teams?

The Premier League players can be any nationality so long as they play for a top flight English club, and the World XI must all play overseas and not for teams in England.

My Premier League XI

1. Goalkeeper
2. Right Back
3. Left Back
4. Centre Back
5. Centre Back
6. Holding Midfielder
7. Midfielder
8. Midfielder
9. Striker
10. Winger/Attacker (left):
11. Winger/Attacker (right):

My World XI

1. Goalkeeper
2. Right Back
3. Left Back
4. Centre Back
5. Centre Back
6. Holding Midfielder
7. Midfielder
8. Midfielder
9. Striker
10. Winger/Attacker (left):
11. Winger/Attacker (right):

To help you, we've put together a list of some of our favourite players in these positions, but remember, this is your team, choose any players you feel will create an epic XI, even if they aren't on this list.

SELECTED PL PLAYERS

GOALKEEPER
Alisson (Liverpool)
Ederson (Manchester City)
Emiliano Martinez (Aston Villa)

RIGHT BACK
Trent Alexander-Arnold (Liverpool)
Kyle Walker (Manchester City)
Reece James (Chelsea)

LEFT BACK
Andy Robertson (Liverpool)
Destiny Udogie (Spurs)
Luke Shaw (Manchester United)

CENTRE BACK
Ruben Dias (Manchester City)
Virgil Van Dijk (Liverpool)
Micky van de Ven (Spurs)
William Saliba (Arsenal)

HOLDING MIDFIELDER
Declan Rice (Arsenal)
Rodri (Manchester City)
Bruno Guimaraes (Newcastle United)

MIDFIELDER
Kevin De Bruyne (Manchester City)
Bruno Fernandes (Manchester United)
Martin Odegaard (Arsenal)
James Maddison (Spurs)

STRIKER
Erling Haaland (Manchester City)
Son Heung-min (Spurs)
Cole Palmer (Chelsea)

WINGER/ATTACKER (LEFT)
Marcus Rashford (Manchester United)
Luis Diaz (Liverpool)
Jack Grealish (Manchester City)

WINGER/ATTACKER (RIGHT)
Mo Salah (Liverpool)
Bukayo Saka (Arsenal)
Dejan Kulusevski (Spurs)

SELECTED WORLD PLAYERS

GOALKEEPER
Marc-Andre Ter Stegen (Barcelona)
Manuel Neuer (Bayern Munich)
Gianluigi Donnarumma (PSG)

RIGHT BACK
Achraf Hakimi (PSG)
Denzel Dumfries (Inter Milan)
Dani Carvajal (Real Madrid)

LEFT BACK
Alphonso Davies (Bayern Munich)
Ferland Mendy (Real Madrid)
Theo Hernandez (AC Milan)

CENTRE BACK
Antonio Rudiger (Real Madrid)
Matthijs de Ligt (Bayern Munich)
David Alaba (Real Madrid)
Ronald Araujo (Barcelona)

HOLDING MIDFIELDER
Aurelien Tchouameni (Real Madrid)
Joshua Kimmich (Bayern Munich)
Eduardo Camavinga (Real Madrid)

MIDFIELDER
Frenkie de Jong (Barcelona)
Toni Kroos (Real Madrid)
Jude Bellingham (Real Madrid)
Leon Goretzka (Bayern Munich)

STRIKER
Harry Kane (Bayern Munich)
Victor Osimhen (Napoli)
Cristiano Ronaldo (Al Nassr)

WINGER/ATTACKER (LEFT)
Vinicius Junior (Real Madrid)
Rafael Leao (AC Milan)
Kingsley Coman (Bayern Munich)

WINGER/ATTACKER (RIGHT)
Rodrygo (Real Madrid)
Leroy Sane (Bayern Munich)
Lionel Messi (Inter Miami)

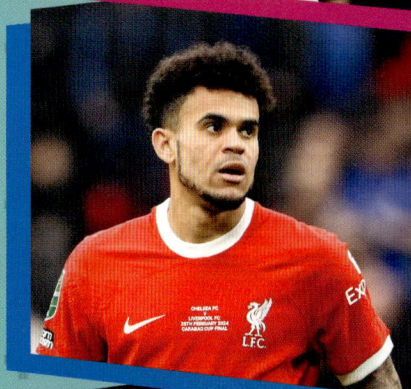

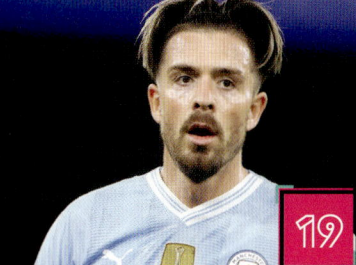

FUTURE STAR
LEWIS MILEY

+ The new kid on the block talks to *SHOOT* about his breakthrough season with his boyhood club, Newcastle United.

How's your first senior season with the Magpies been?

"It's a bit mental! I wasn't expecting to play so many games in a quick period of time, to be honest. I've always just tried to treat them like any other game, really. That's what you've got to do. I feel like I've been doing well. I've just been enjoying it really. That's the main thing you've got to do I think. Just enjoy it and play your way. Not many people get to have this opportunity, playing at the top level for the first time. I've just got to keep enjoying it."

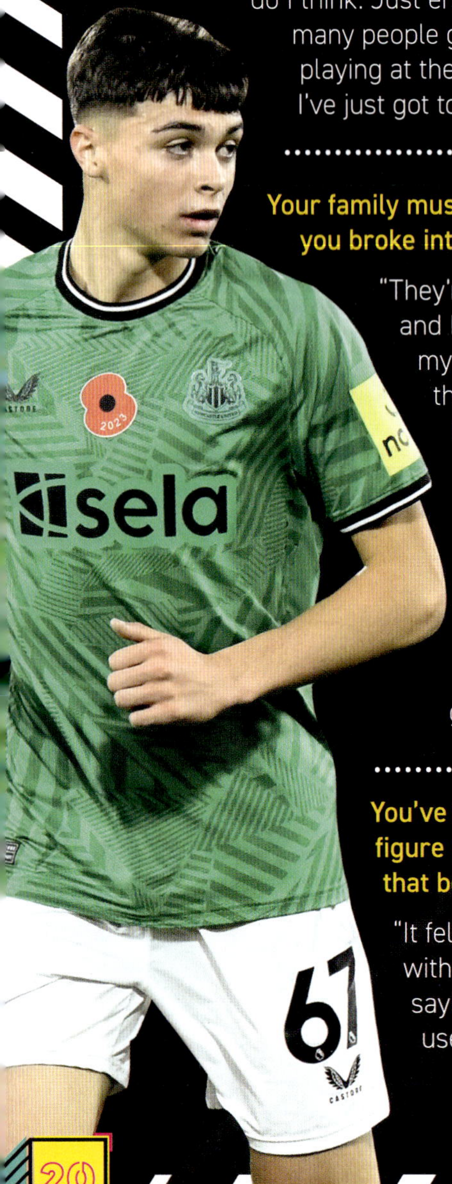

Your family must have been thrilled when you broke into the team?

"They're all buzzing, to be honest, and I think they're buzzing with my performances so far. They think that I've done well, so I've got to keep it up. My mum and dad always believed in me. They've said during the years they've always believed in us – and I've always done the same really. I've just kept playing football and got to this position."

You've become a well-known figure pretty quickly – what's that been like?

"It felt a bit weird at first with people coming up and saying my name, but I'm used to it now."

How's your autograph signing coming along?

"I've been practising it, yeah. It's actually alright now, to be fair!"

Coming into such a big team with great players aged 17 wasn't easy – how do you keep calm?

"I'd say just know your job and stuff in the game. That'll take care of itself, and you'll be able to enjoy it on the other side. You just have to take it in your stride, really, and just be composed."

FACT FILE
CLUB: Newcastle United
TURNED PRO: 2023
COUNTRY: England
POSITION: Midfielder
BORN: 1 May 2006

You've not long left school – were you a good student or did you just want to play football all the time?

"I enjoyed school - sometimes! It was a bit boring, but I just got through it really. I liked all my teachers – they were all supportive, and when I was going through school obviously I used to come in and out of school for football, and they were all good with me."

How do you keep your feet on the ground?

"I don't let myself get too high or too low. I just stay in the middle. You've got to play to your strengths, really, and keep working on the things you need to work on."

You signed a long new term contract at the start of 2024 – that must have been a big moment for you?

"It was a really proud moment for me and my family to sign another professional contract with my boyhood club. I couldn't be prouder. Hopefully I can continue to do well over the next few years, and I can keep improving my performance and getting better as a player."

And finally, what's it like playing in front of the fans you used to stand among as a kid?

"It's a real joy playing in front of the Newcastle United fans, especially to hear them chanting my name. Their support means so much to me and my family, and I'm looking forward to the future."

SPOT THE BOSS

There are ten football managers in this crowd scene – all of them on a scouting mission – but can you spot them all?

- Pep Guardiola ○
- Gareth Southgate ○
- Carlo Ancelotti ○
- Mikel Arteta ○
- Unai Emery ○
- Erik ten Hag ○
- Marco Silva ○
- Maurcio Pochetinno ○
- Xabi Alonso ○
- Ange Postecoglou ○

ANSWERS ON PAGES 76-77

SHOOT's FOOTBALL A to Z QUIZ

26 letters, 26 questions, how well will you do with Shoot's A-Z football quiz? Check your rating at the bottom of the page!

A Birmingham club who's first and last letter is this.

B Sheffield United's nickname.

C Part of a club name shared by these clubs – Manchester, Leicester, Coventry and Bristol.

D John Stones, Ben White, Virgil van Dijk and Fabian Schar play this position.

E Liverpool's local rivals.

F Country PSG's Ousmane Dembele represents.

G Arsenal's nickname.

H Score three goals in a game and you've got one of these.

I Bournemouth's Spanish boss, Andoni...

J Bowen – England and West Ham's livewire forward.

K Tottenham's Swedish winger Dejan...

L Lionesses and Arsenal captain Williamson.

M What you don't want to do in a penalty shoot-out.

N The orange wearing European football crazy nation!

O
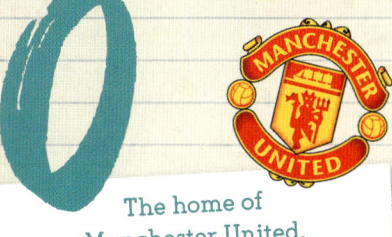
The home of Manchester United.

P
Get fouled in the area and the referee will award a...

Q

Club Eberechi Eze played for before Crystal Palace.

R

Andy, the attacking Liverpool and Scotland left-back.

S

The name of this football Annual you are reading.

T
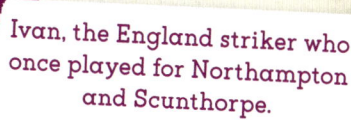
Ivan, the England striker who once played for Northampton and Scunthorpe.

U
Sheffield, Manchester, Leeds, West Ham, and Newcastle share this name.

V

Micky, the Spurs defender who is one of the fastest in the Premier League.

W

Premier League side who play in a gold and black kit.

X

Granit – the former Arsenal skipper who moved to play for Bayer Leverkusen.

Y
Get two of these cards and you will be sent off.

Z

Wilfried, the former Crystal Palace winger who moved to play in Turkey.

YOUR SCORE

0-10
Are you sure you're even trying! Time to watch more football and do the quiz again!

11-20
A very respectable score, you know your stuff, a decent effort!

21-26
WOW!! Mega-fan alert! Time to bring out your favourite goal celebration!

ANSWERS ON PAGES 76-77

NEW KIDS ON THE BLOCK

Every season a new crop of talented young stars make the breakthrough and challenge the best players around. Here are nine up and coming young stars who are already making a big impression with their clubs.

KOBBIE MAINOO

DATE OF BIRTH: 19 April 2005

This defensive midfielder has already become a first-team regular with United and won a call-up to the senior England squad in 2024, aged only 18. Plays with a maturity beyond his years and is destined to be a huge star for club and country.

LEWIS MILEY

DATE OF BIRTH: 1 May 2006

Exciting midfield talent who broke into the Newcastle United side aged only 17 and became a first team regular throughout 2023/24. A clever, inventive player who has huge promise, Miley is set for big things in 2025 with the Magpies.

RICO LEWIS

DATE OF BIRTH: 21 November 2004

The versatile City youngster is already making waves in international football. Able to play as a full-back on either flank but is perhaps at his best when he is in central midfield and can use his boundless energy to maximum effect.

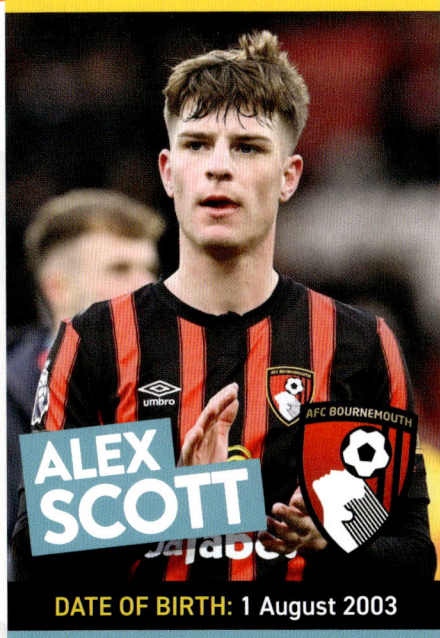

ALEX SCOTT

DATE OF BIRTH: 1 August 2003

Nicknamed the 'Guernsey Grealish', the skilful Alex Scott will be a star that will rise and rise. After earning a glowing reputation at Bristol City, the gifted playmaker enhanced his reputation further with an outstanding performance against Manchester City and joined Bournemouth in 2023.

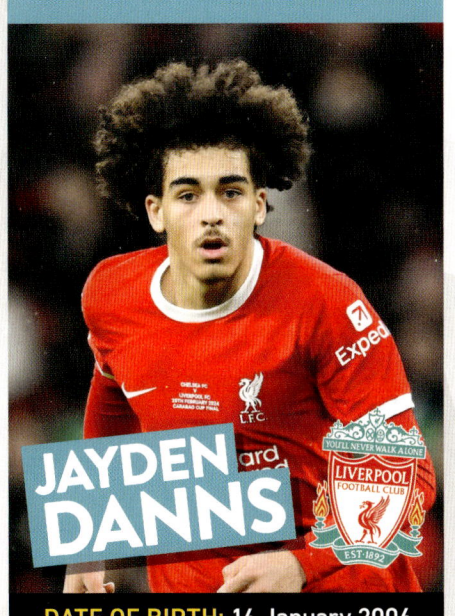

JAYDEN DANNS

DATE OF BIRTH: 16 January 2006

The Red's exciting young forward has the happy knack of making things happen and having a big impact. Danns is the latest in a long line of promising youngsters at Anfield. He is quick, strong and a handful for any defender, so we expect to see Jayden more and more in 2025 across all the competitions for Liverpool.

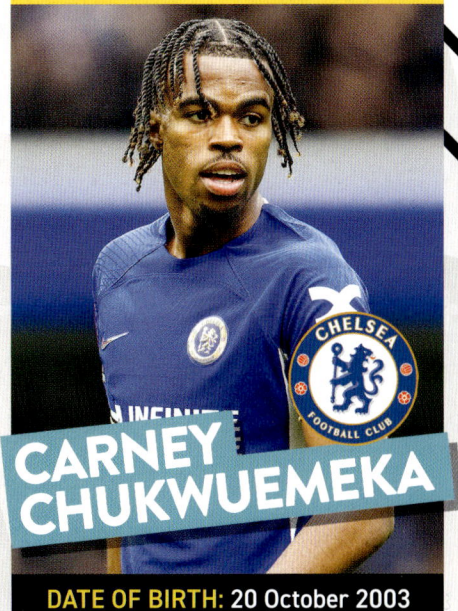

CARNEY CHUKWUEMEKA

DATE OF BIRTH: 20 October 2003

A powerful and athletic attacking midfielder who can also play on the wing, Carney Chukwuemeka is a rising star at Chelsea who will be a key player in their future success and bring silverware back to The Bridge. Fearless going forward, he is also tall and uses his physicality to great effect.

JADEN PHILOGENE

DATE OF BIRTH: 8 February 2002

He may be the oldest on the list, but this immense talent has had to drop down to the Championship to really find his feet. A gifted winger who has the ability to beat players with ease, Philogene may have to leave Hull to get back to the Premier League — but he will end up there, sooner or later.

NONI MADUEKE

DATE OF BIRTH: 10 March 2002

Like team-mate Carney Chukwuemeka, Noni Madueke is a fast, powerful, and imposing attacking midfielder or winger. His direct approach and all-action style have made him a big favourite among the Chelsea fans already. His electric pace and dribbling ability will cause problems for any defenders he comes up against.

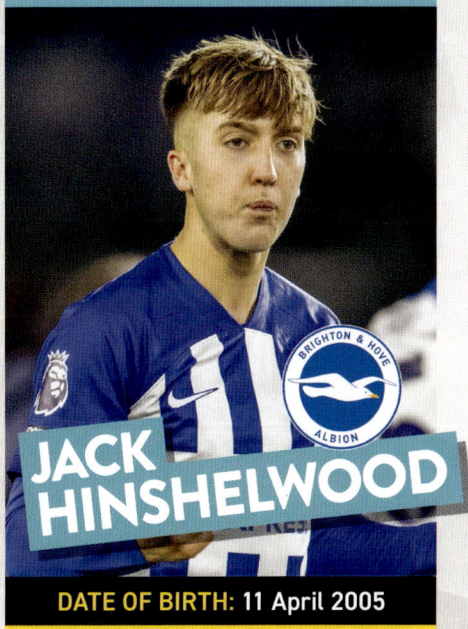

JACK HINSHELWOOD

DATE OF BIRTH: 11 April 2005

Another teenage talent who can play in several positions with equal effect, Jack Hinshelwood is quickly earning a reputation as one of Brighton's brightest prospects. Able to slot in defence if needed, he is primarily a play-making midfielder with excellent vision and an eye for goal.

FUTURE STAR

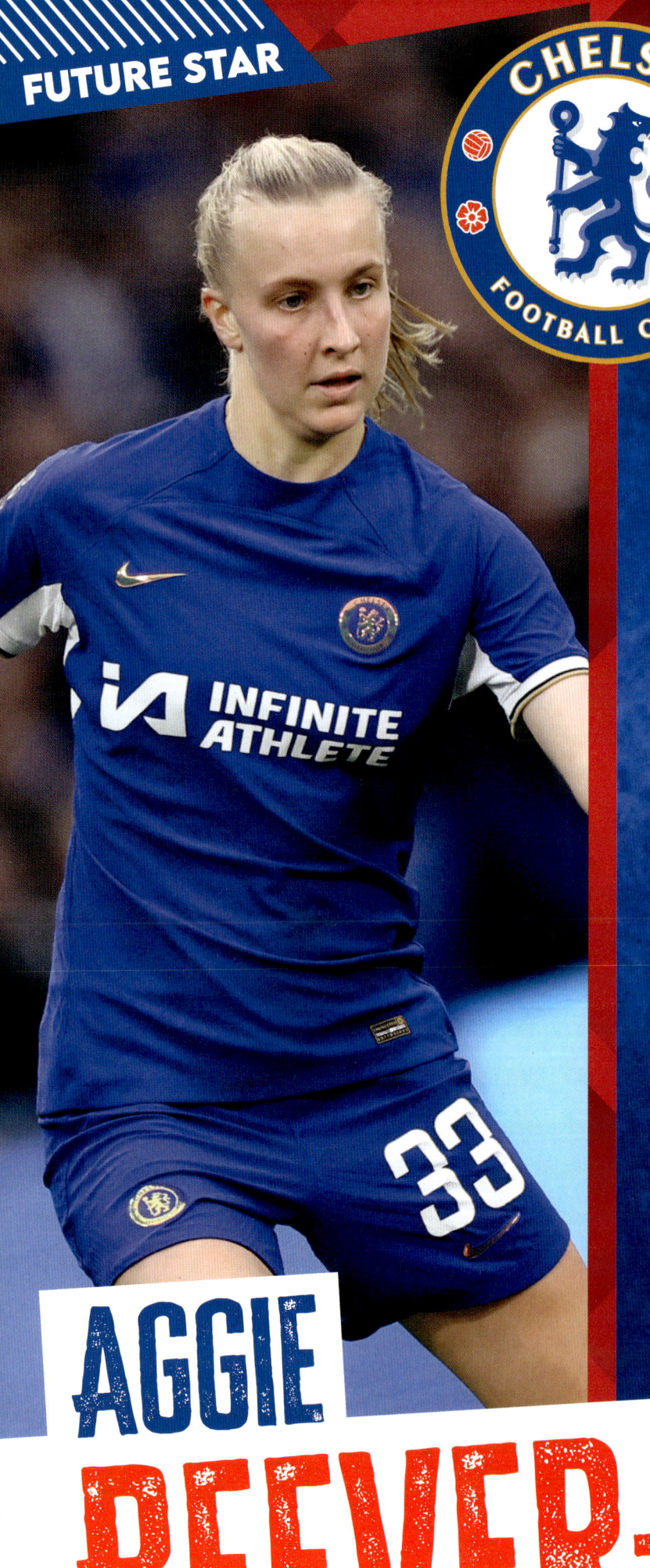

One of the WSL's up and coming talents spoke exclusively to *SHOOT* as she answers our Q&A...

How did your love of football start?
"Through my grandad. He used to take me to a few of the games at Stamford Bridge. That's where it really started."

Do you recall how you first started playing?
"My mum and dad signed me up for a local little league down at the local park and I played in goal with the boys. I think it was a 'You're a girl, let's chuck you in goal', then I think I came outfield for one day and I haven't looked back since."

So you didn't want to be a goalkeeper?
"When you're a kid who has that much energy, you're just running round. But I've always been an attack-minded player, wanting to get on the ball and dribble a lot and that's probably where it started when I was younger – dribbling and trying to score."

You were scouted by Chelsea - how did that happen and did it go well?
"A Chelsea scout said to my dad, 'Your girl isn't too bad is she, you should send her down for a trial.' I had my first trial at Chelsea when I was maybe eight or nine, and I didn't get in the first year. It felt like the end of the world!"

But you didn't give up...
"No! I remember the coach, told me what I needed to work on and then I came back, tried out again the next year and I got in. I think I then signed when I was nine or 10 and I've been there ever since."

AGGIE BEEVER-JONES

Then you were loaned to Everton?

"Yeah, Everton helped out massively as well, they gave me that trust and game time I needed. I always look back on both clubs with very fond memories and thank both coaches because they've helped me a lot."

Your loan spells really helped, and you had a wonderful 2023/24 season with Chelsea - what was it like playing at Stamford Bridge?

"Stamford Bridge definitely feels like a home away from home. We have Kingsmeadow which we've made our fortress and we have such a good atmosphere there. At Stamford Bridge, you can see that happening slowly but surely, we are getting more and more fans there and the atmosphere feels amazing."

Your best advice to youngsters?

"Play with a smile on your face, which is what my mum and dad have always said to me, so I try and do that!"

You turned professional when you were 18 - what was that like when you were told?

"I trained a few times and played a few training games, and I thought I did alright so I always had hopes, but I never really thought it would happen. Then, I remember getting called into the room and Paul [Green] and Emma [Hayes] said, 'We'd love to offer you a contract'.

What did you do first after that?

"I called my mum and dad like 'you won't believe it, it's actually happened'. They're both Chelsea fans and were as ecstatic as I was. I was so shaky the whole journey home. It was a very proud time of my life and I'll always be grateful to them for trusting me to give me that contract."

Your first involvement actually came on loan with Bristol City, didn't it?

"Bristol City took me in with open arms when I was 18 years-old with not much experience really in Championship football. They welcomed me like I was one of their own and helped me in many ways both on and off the pitch, with living away from home and getting the support I needed.

"Then on the pitch, they trusted me to play, which as a younger player, is something you really need. You need that game time to experiment, try new things and make mistakes. I was able to do that at Bristol City."

FACT FILE

CLUB: Chelsea
TURNED PRO: 2020
COUNTRY: England
POSITION: Forward
BORN: 27 July 2003

SUPER TALL!

Depending on which position you play, towering over everyone on the pitch has it's advantages! Here are the five Premier League stars who are taller than everyone else.

LUCAS BERGSTROM

6FT 7"

The Finnish keeper is always going to be favourite in an aerial challenge with his arm reach and jump probably equalling something like nine feet!

DAN BURN

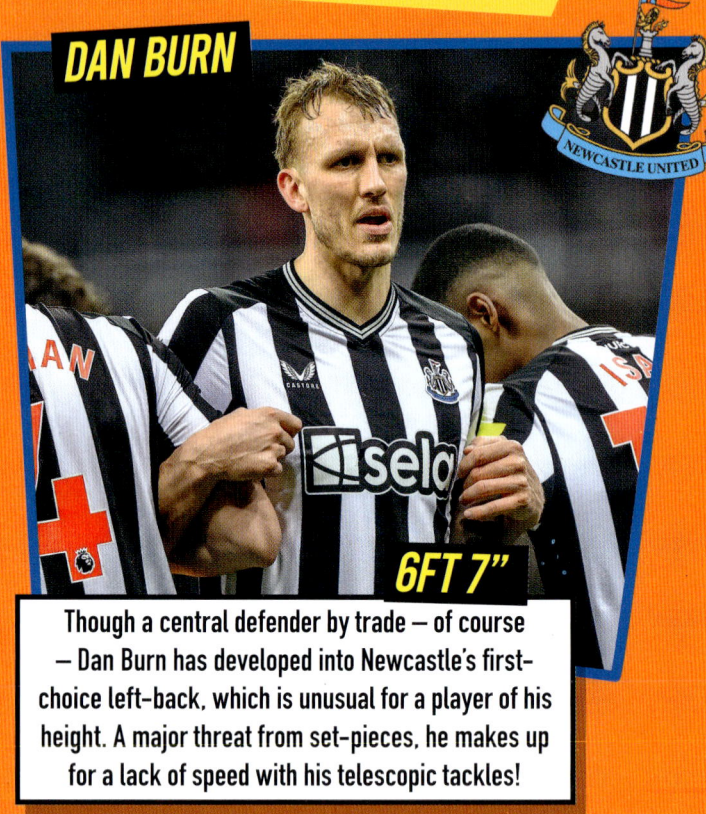

6FT 7"

Though a central defender by trade — of course — Dan Burn has developed into Newcastle's first-choice left-back, which is unusual for a player of his height. A major threat from set-pieces, he makes up for a lack of speed with his telescopic tackles!

FRASER FORSTER

6FT 7"

Much-travelled Forster has turned his height to his advantage. It's not always easy for tall keepers to get down and block low shots, but almost 500 career games proves he has overcome that issue and flourished.

NICK POPE

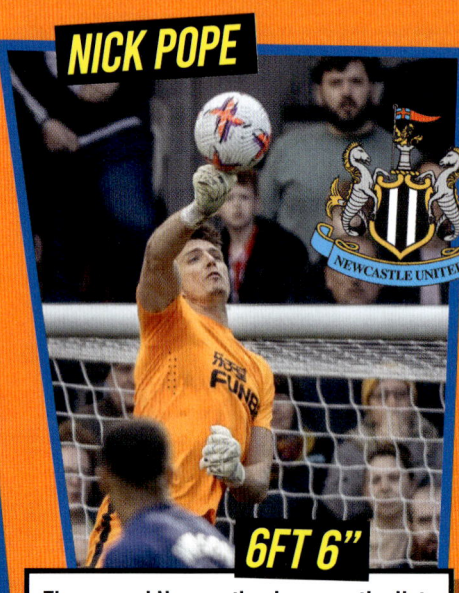

6FT 6"

The second Newcastle player on the list is also another goalkeeper in our top five. The England stopper is rated as one of the best in the Premier League and uses his height to great effect on opposition set-pieces and crosses.

KRISTOFFER AJER

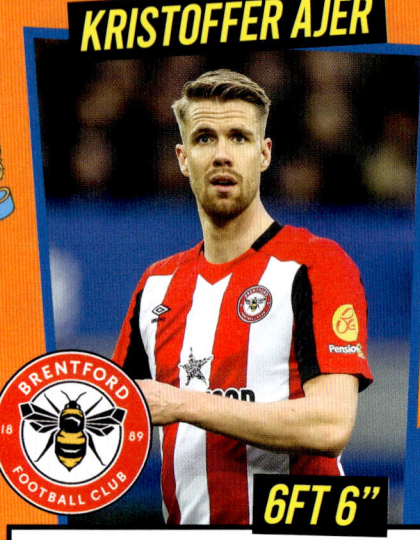

6FT 6"

The Brentford centre-half is probably the only Premier League defender who could mark Dan Burn comfortably! The Norwegian is a formidable figure and was very tall from a very early age, once scoring 26 goals in one game as a kid!

SUPER FAST!

It's not just tall players that have an advantage on the pitch, being super speedy can cause the opposition problems too. Below are our top five Premier League speed demons!

MICKY VAN DE VEN

23.23 MPH

Superfast and an excellent timer of tackles, the Dutch defender has proved a superb signing for Tottenham — and is proving a nightmare for Premier League strikers. He's so fast he could run from one side of London to the other in under an hour!

KYLE WALKER

23.18 MPH

Coming at a fraction less fast than Micky van de Ven is Manchester City and England star Kyle Walker. Blessed with frightening pace, there are few in the Premier League who can get away from this speedy right-back.

CHIEDOZIE OGBENE

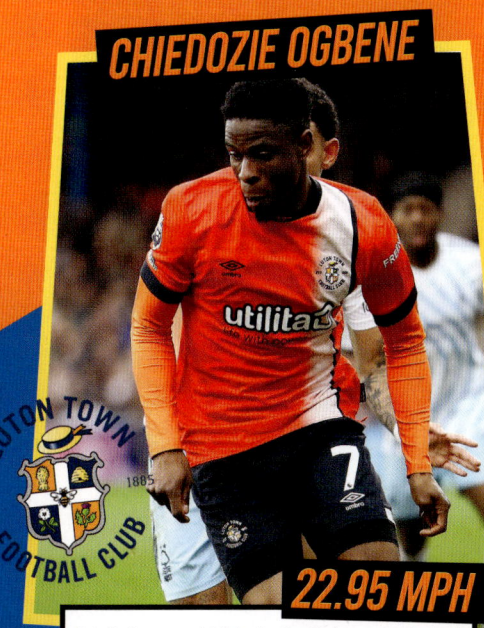

22.95 MPH

Irish forward Chiedozie Ogbene enjoyed a productive 2023/24 campaign in the PL with his lightning pace a huge plus for Luton Town. A pacy, tricky winger who uses his speed to great effect.

PEDRO NETO

22.90 MPH

Fast, tricky, and skilful, Pedro is one of the best wingers in the Premier League. The Portuguese star creates many assists with his pace by leaving defenders behind. His intelligence of knowing what to do next makes him a standout talent.

DOMINIK SZOBOSZLAI

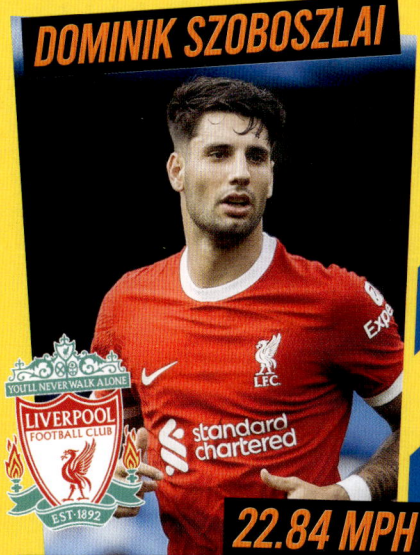

22.84 MPH

It is unusual for a fast player to be a midfielder, but the Hungarian star is an exception to the rule. Able to burst forward and turn on the after-burners, he is a huge asset to Liverpool and can effortlessly charge from box to box!

RECORD BREAKERS

The Premier League began life in 1992 and there have been many great players during that time. But who are the best of the best in terms of records and stats? *SHOOT* has gathered all the Premier League data we could find, and here are the results.

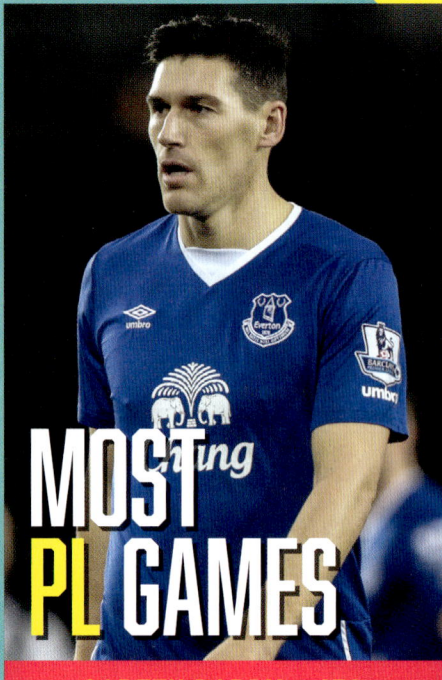

MOST PL GAMES

GARETH BARRY – 653

The former Aston Villa, Manchester City and Everton midfielder leads the way — so far! He clocked up 653 appearances during his career — but James Milner is on his trail! As of the end of the 2023/24 PL season, Milner was just 13 games behind his old Villa and City teammate!

MOST PL CLUBS

MARCUS BENT – 8

When it comes to a player who travelled up and down the land playing for teams during his career, Marcus tops the list with EIGHT different clubs! Bent played for Crystal Palace, Blackburn Rovers, Ipswich Town, Leicester City, Everton, Charlton Athletic, Wigan Athletic, and Wolverhampton Wanderers. If you include clubs outside the top flight, the total is 18!

YOUNGEST PL PLAYER

ETHAN NWANERI
15 YEARS AND 181 DAYS

The youngest player ever to play in the top flight is Ethan Nwaneri who was 15 years and 181 days old when he played for Arsenal v Brentford in September 2022.

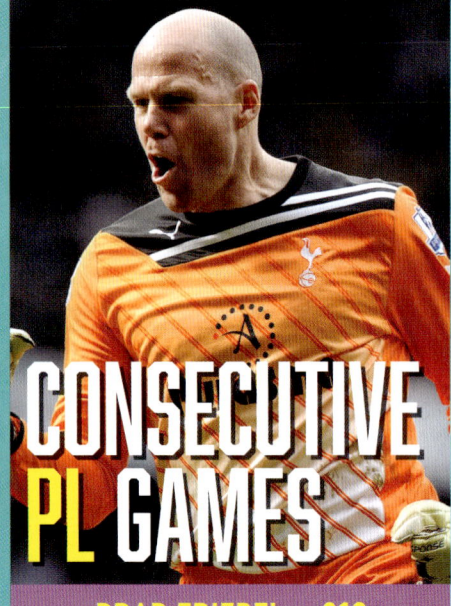

CONSECUTIVE PL GAMES

BRAD FRIEDEL — 310

Consistency, form and avoiding injury are key to playing regularly, but nobody can match the record of American goalkeeper Brad Friedel who played 310 Premier League games in a row during spells at Blackburn Rovers, Aston Villa and Tottenham Hotspur in an incredible eight-year period. Imagine being the No.2 keeper during that time!

OLDEST PL PLAYER

JOHN BURRIDGE
43 YEARS, 162 DAYS

In May 1995, John Burridge claimed the record for being the oldest player to play in the PL when he turned out for Manchester City v QPR. He started his career in 1969 and hung up his gloves in 1997 — that's almost 30 years. Wow!

PL SUPER SUB

JAMES MILNER — 200+

James Milner has made more than 600 appearances during his Premier League career for Leeds United, Newcastle, Aston Villa, Manchester City, Liverpool and Brighton — but did you know one third were as a sub? That's an incredible (and little known) fact to impress your pals with!

TOP 5: MOST PL APPEARANCES

MOST PL SEASONS

JAMES MILNER – 23 SEASONS

James Milner has played in every PL campaign from 2002/03 to 2024/25 — that's an incredible 23 seasons at the very top of English football! In that time he has won three Premier League titles, two FA Cups, two League Cups and two Community Shields, not to mention successes in Europe. He keeps himself in such good shape that we may see him playing in a 24th season, or even a 25th!

PL GOALSCORING FEATS!

Most Premier League goals: ALAN SHEARER – 260
Most Premier League goals at one club: HARRY KANE (Tottenham Hotspur) — 213
Most Premier League hat-tricks: SERGIO AGUERO (Manchester City) – 12
Oldest goal-scorer: TEDDY SHERINGHAM – 40 YEARS AND 268 DAYS
Youngest goal-scorer: JAMES VAUGHAN – 16 YEARS AND 271 DAYS
Most consecutive PL matches scored in: JAMIE VARDY – 11 GAMES (SCORED 13 GOALS)

RANK	PLAYER	GAMES	POSITION	FIRST SEASON	LAST SEASON
1	GARETH BARRY	653	MIDFIELDER	1997–98	2017–18
2	JAMES MILNER	640	MIDFIELDER	2002–03	STILL PLAYING
3	RYAN GIGGS	632	MIDFIELDER	1992–93	2013–14
4	FRANK LAMPARD	609	MIDFIELDER	1995–96	2014–15
5	DAVID JAMES	572	GOALKEEPER	1992–93	2009–10

BADGE MASH-UP!

Let's mix things up a little! We've created four club badges from teams in the Premier League, Bundesliga, La Liga and Serie A to make four unique mega badges – all you have to do is figure out the club badges that make up these mix-ups!

Remember, there are four clubs to find in each badge – good luck!

BADGE 1

BADGE 2

BADGE 3

BADGE 4

YOUR ANSWERS

BADGE 1
Premier League: _____
Bundesliga: _____
La Liga: _____
Serie A: _____

BADGE 2
Premier League: _____
Bundesliga: _____
La Liga: _____
Serie A: _____

BADGE 3
Premier League: _____
Bundesliga: _____
La Liga: _____
Serie A: _____

BADGE 4
Premier League: _____
Bundesliga: _____
La Liga: _____
Serie A: _____

ANSWERS ON PAGES 76-77

BADGE TRUE OR FALSE?

How well do you know what clubs have on their badge? Can you figure out whether the 12 statements below are true or false?

1. Newcastle United have a magpie on their club badge.

2. Atletico Madrid have a bear on their club badge.

3. Brighton have a seagull on their club badge.

4. Inter Miami have flamingos on their club badge.

5. Brentford have a large bee on their badge.

6. Barcelona have a gold crown on their club badge.

7. Ipswich Town have a red tractor on their club badge.

8. England have four lions on their badge.

9. Leeds United have a red rose on their club badge.

10. Brazil have five stars on their badge.

11. Aston Villa have a lion on their club badge.

12. Manchester United and Manchester City both have a ship on their club badge.

ANSWERS ON PAGES 76-77

FUTURE STAR

One of *SHOOT's* up and coming talents for 2025 is Manchester United and England midfielder Kobbie Mainoo – here, he answers our Q&A...

First things first, Kobbie - how do you correctly pronounce your name?

"Kobbie [Kob-ee] Mainoo [May-new]."

Do you have a nickname?

"A lot of people call me Kobs, yeah. Kobs."

Was it football all the way as a kid?

"Football was literally my whole childhood, I guess. I mean, from as long as I can remember, it was always playing football throughout the week: on the weekends, at school, wherever. At home, in the living room. As much as my mum hated it! It was just my whole childhood, pretty much."

Who is your all-time Manchester United favourite?

"I'd say Paul Scholes. His passing, his movement, the way he could finish. His intelligence, yeah, he was a great player."

Who would you say is your role model?

"I can't say that I have one. I like to pick different things from different people, When it's football players, I pick different things from their games to try and add to mine and stuff. So I wouldn't say I follow one person directly. I just try to pick up things as much as I can from other people."

KOBBIE MAINOO

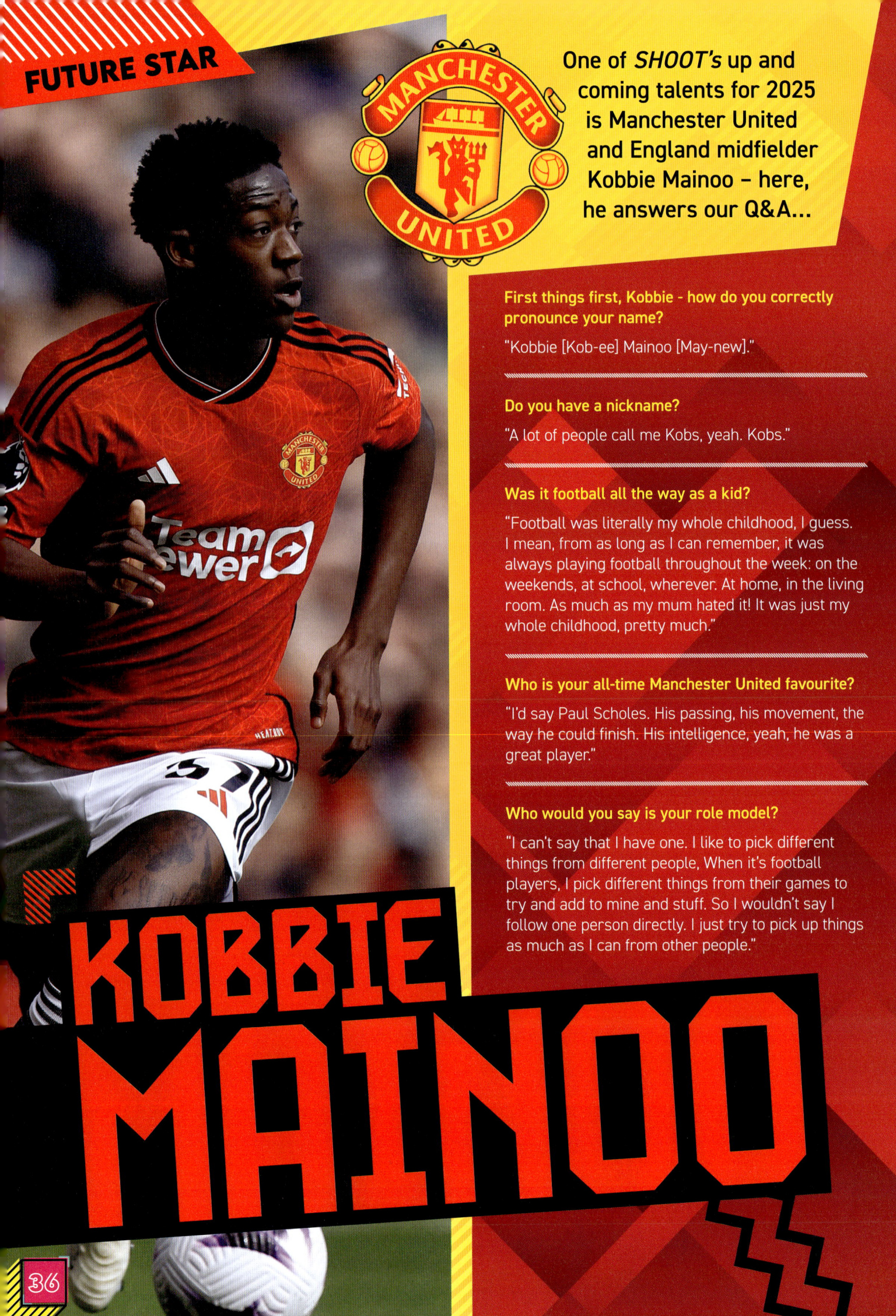

Which type of music you listen to?
"I like Drake at the moment. A lot of old Drake stuff, like the slower stuff. The more chilled stuff before a game. I don't really like to get hyped before games. I like to just relax."

If you could pick one skill attribute of any other United player what skill would it be and why?
"Maybe Marcus Rashford's speed - he's rapid isn't he?"

What other sports do you watch in your spare time?
"I follow boxing. I like UFC as well. Basketball, there's a few. Yeah, there are a few sports that I like, but with the times, especially with the American sports, the time difference mean it's tough to stay up to watch, but I try to follow them as closely as I can."

Finally, what advice do you have for youngsters hoping to follow in your footsteps?
"I'd say just try and be consistent with how you play, no matter who you're playing with or who you're playing against, just try and play. Play your game and not let things going wrong or things going against you discourage you. And I think that's the main thing you can do. Just worry about things that are in your control and keep trying to do the right things."

For your age, you have so much composure on the ball – where does that come from?
"I don't know! I mean I've always felt most comfortable when I'm on the ball. I feel like it's when I'm in control."

What are the drills you did as a kid that you enjoyed the most?
"Futsal really helped. I mean just having the ball at the feet as much as possible and always having to be checking your shoulders for players coming and stuff like that. So that definitely helped."

Why do you wear the number 37?
"It's the number, I was given. I didn't really have a choice! I mean, last season, I was 73 and, to be honest, I didn't really mind what number I changed to this season. Just give me 37."

When did you first realise you wanted to be a footballer?
"I don't remember. I mean I just remember always having the ball at my feet, so it just seemed like there was only one path. Yeah, I thought I'm pretty good at this so I might as well carry on. It was always going to be that."

What is your favourite United moment – can you remember the first game you went to at Old Trafford?
"I don't remember my first game. Favourite United moment? Maybe Rooney's overhead kick. I remember seeing that against City."

FACT FILE
CLUB: Manchester United
TURNED PRO: 2022
COUNTRY: England
POSITION: Midfielder
BORN: 19 April 2005

SUPERSTAR SUPERCAR

It doesn't matter how many goals, trophies or social media followers a player has, they are not a football superstar without an epic footballer's supercar! Here are some of the flashiest cars driven by the games flashiest players!

ERLING HAALAND

BUGATTI CHIRON
This speedster is perfect for a goal machine like Manchester City's number 9 — but a car like this will set you back a cool £2.3m!

NEYMAR JR

ROLLS ROYCE GHOST
Compared with some of the car in this list, the £270,000 price tag is quite cheap, so this is probably this one Neymar uses to nip to the shops in!

CRISTIANO RONALDO

FERRARI DAYTONA SP3
The Portuguese legend drives a car that matches his style — classy and fast. £1.7m will get you one of these beauties!

GABRIEL MARTINELLI

LAMBORGHINI URUS
Arsenal's Brazilian winger zips around North London in this stylish four litre twin turbo that costs around £220,000.

KEVIN DE BRUYNE

LAMBORGHINI AVENTADOR
The ultimate pass master will almost certainly pass you in this super-charged beast! A cool £400,000 would buy this speedster!

MO SALAH

BENTLEY CONTINENTAL GT
The Egyptian King drives like a king in this grand Bentley — not sure if his pet cats would get a ride, but at £160,000, it's one of the more affordable motors in this list!

BRUNO GUIMARAES

MERCEDES AMG G63
Bruno has a stylish car to match his stylish play, and at around £132,000, it's reasonably priced for a smart-looking family car.

LEWIS DUNK

CLUB: Brighton & Hove Albion
COUNTRY: England
POSITION: Defender
BORN: 21 November 1991
PREVIOUS CLUBS: Bognor Regis Town (loan), Bristol City (loan)

DID YOU KNOW?

Although Lewis is the Brighton captain, the team he supported growing up was Chelsea, and he named his family dog 'Didier' in homage to Chelsea forward Didier Drogba.

NEW KIDS ON THE BLOCK

WOMEN'S SUPER LEAGUE

SHOOT's scouts have been out and about checking out the most promising youngsters in the FA Women's Super League – and here's nine we reckon will become big stars in the coming year.

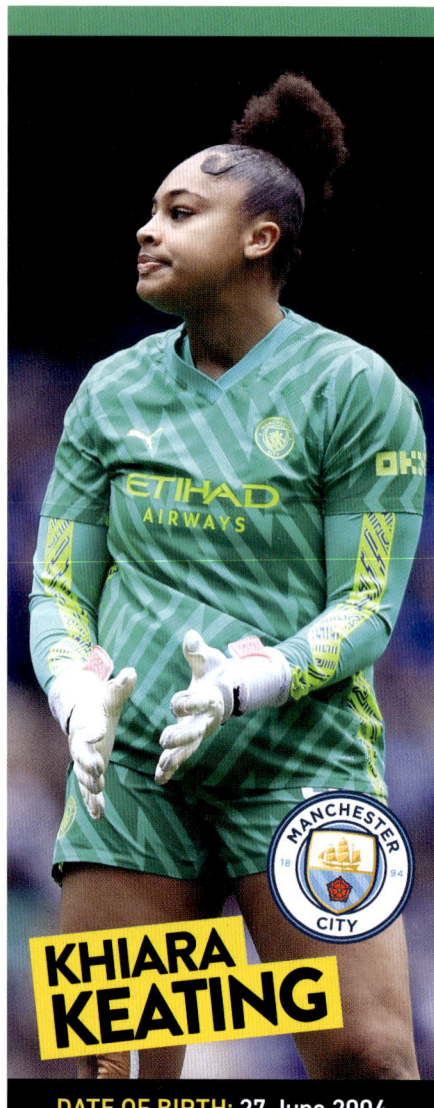

KHIARA KEATING

DATE OF BIRTH: 27 June 2004

Already established as Manchester City's No.1 – and broken into the England squad – Khiara Keating looks set for big things. Athletic and agile, she is capable of spectacular saves and has excellent reflexes.

GRACE CLINTON

DATE OF BIRTH: 31 March 2003

Grace Clinton was allowed to join Spurs on a season-long loan in 2023/24, which proved to be an inspired decision by United as the combative midfielder shone in North London and will be a big asset for United and England in 2025.

BROOKE ASPIN

DATE OF BIRTH: 1 July 2005

Big things are expected of the Chelsea defender. Brooke spent the 2023/24 campaign with Bristol City and made a huge impact – and returned to her parent club for the 2024/25 season. The strong, reliable defender has a big future with the Blues.

JESS PARK

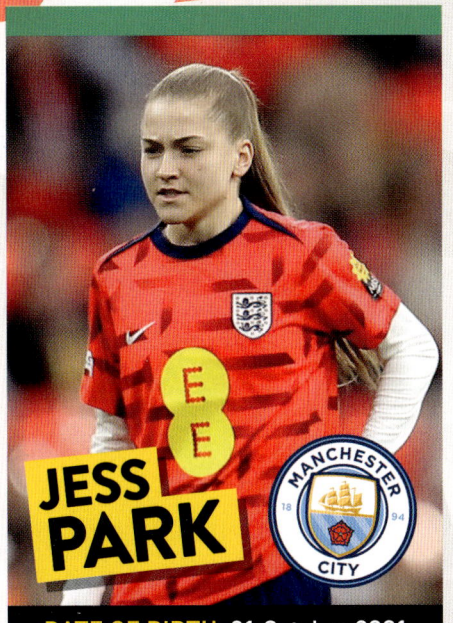

DATE OF BIRTH: 21 October 2001

Jess Park has had to be patient waiting for a chance to shine at Manchester City, and she had to spend a season with Everton on loan to get the minutes she needed to progress. But having returned to City, this talented playmaker, with an eye for goal, is starting to really blossom.

AGGIE BEEVER-JONES

DATE OF BIRTH: 27 July 2003

Much like the Chelsea men's team, the Chelsea women's team make excellent use of the loan system — and Aggie Beever-Jones is yet another example. The young forward spent the past two seasons with Bristol City and Everton on loan but will be fighting for a place in Chelsea's squad — and England 2025.

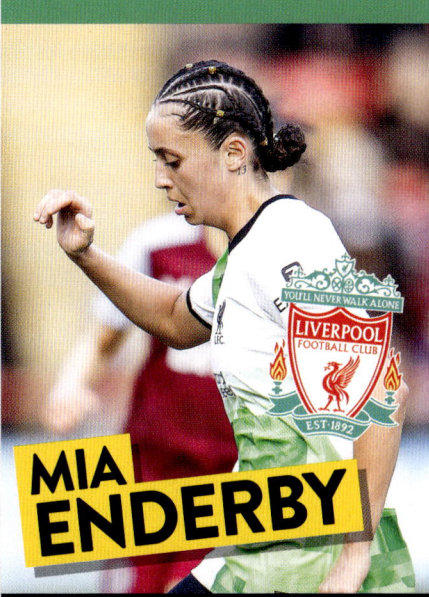

MIA ENDERBY

DATE OF BIRTH: 31 May 2005

An explosive young talent, Mia Enderby is a fast, exciting winger who has made a big impression at Liverpool. A fan favourite, she loves to run at defenders and create chances for her teammates as well as get on the scoresheet herself. Mia is definitely a WSL player to watch out for in 2025!

MISSY GOODWIN

DATE OF BIRTH: 27 January 2003

An inventive and quick-thinking forward, Missy Goodwin is another exciting prospect who has caught the eye. Sharp, speedy and energetic, she is expected to kick on in 2025 and force her way into England squad contention just in time for the UEFA European Women's Championship.

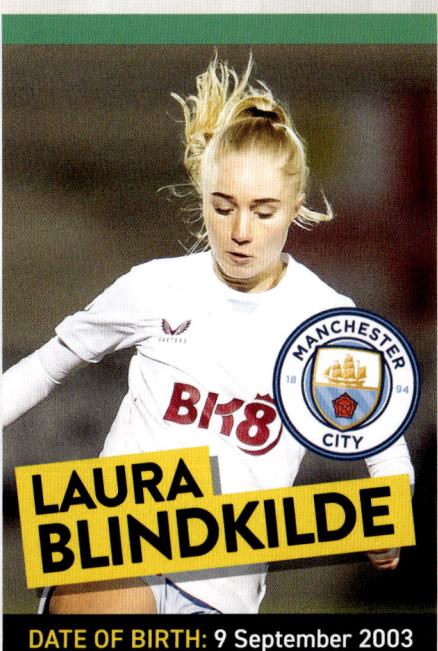

LAURA BLINDKILDE

DATE OF BIRTH: 9 September 2003

Manchester City moved quickly to snap up the exciting Laura Blindkilde in the January 2024 transfer window. The attacking midfielder joined the Blues from Aston Villa and is tipped by many as 'one for the future' — she will get her chance to prove that in City's talented squad.

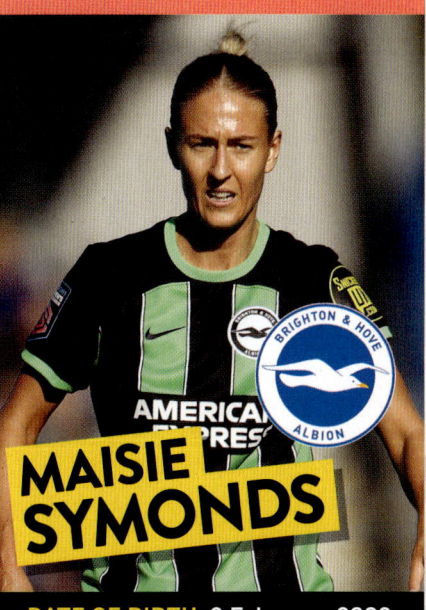

MAISIE SYMONDS

DATE OF BIRTH: 2 February 2003

England U19 captain Maisie has a bright future. A hard-working midfielder, she is a class act in possession and never stops working for her team. Symonds overcame a serious health issue and fought her way back into the Seagulls' team where she is now considered one of their brightest prospects.

BETH MEAD

SHOOT sat down for a Q&A with the exciting Arsenal and Lionesses winger...

Tell us your earliest footballing memory?

It would be when I was six years old and the first time I went to a football session. It was in my local village in Hinderwell, and my Mum took me to get rid of a load of energy. It was all boys there and when my Mum asked if it was alright for me to get involved, the coach said: 'Of course she is but the boys are a little bit rough. Will she be alright?' When my Mum returned an hour later, the guy was like: 'Beth was rougher than the boys and she is a good footballer'. He told me to go further afield towards Middlesbrough, which was a 45-minute drive, and that set up my path because I went to an academy there and worked my way up the ranks.

How would you describe yourself?

I'm quite an energetic, bubbly person, and I think it's always sometimes nice for other people to get that energy when they haven't got it. And I feel like that makes me feel good if I can make somebody else feel good. So I would probably say that part of my personality.

You suffered a really serious ACL injury – what was it like when you came back after such a long time out?

It was at the Emirates in font of 35,000 people and they all went mad when I came on as a sub – it was quite emotional for me, actually, but good to return on the pitch where I was injured in the first place.

What's your biggest achievement?

It would have to be the Euros. Winning the tournament, being named player of the tournament and getting the Golden Boot – I'm not sure I will top that one.

What's your worst habit?

Biting my nails. I don't do it as much as I used to, but I do it more when I'm either stressed or anxious. It is clearly a go-to which I need to still get out of the habit of doing but I am a lot better than I used to be.

Who has been your biggest influence?

It has to be my parents, my Mum, and my Dad. I wouldn't be where I am now had they not pushed me out of my comfort zone, made me do things I didn't want to do, and taken me to every training session, every game, as obviously I couldn't drive as a kid.

Which podcast are you obsessed with?

I love Peter Crouch's. He's good fun and I love hearing his stories from over the years.

Any songs you like to get you ready before a match?

Leah Williamson, our changing room DJ, likes to put on songs to please us all. We love a good upbeat ABBA number though, especially for Swedish player Stina Blackstenius.

What reminds you of home?

Countryside and the beach. I live in the middle of nowhere, right next to a cove of a beach. Also, my local town is very well known for fish and chips - Whitby. So probably that as well.

What's your favourite place in the world?

Probably on a football pitch where my family is – playing football with my family there. They're my two favourite things in the world.

What's your most valuable possession?

It would be my Mum's wedding ring. I carry it everywhere with me now. She is not with us anymore, so it is priceless to me.

What's your advice to youngsters?

"I'd say play with no fear. I started playing against boys when I was six and I quickly built my confidence and ability. If it's something you enjoy doing you should go for it! More women's games being on TV really encourages people – I think it did a few years ago with the World Cup and Euros. We need to continue to support and encourage girls!"

FACT FILE

CLUB: Arsenal
COUNTRY: England
POSITION: Winger/Forward
BORN: 9 May 1995
BIRTHPLACE: Whitby, North Yorkshire
PREVIOUS CLUBS: Sunderland

43

WHO IS THE GOAT?

So, who is the greatest footballer of all time? Four names are mentioned more than any other, but who has the best stats of all? Using our unique points scoring system, *SHOOT* have devised a way of figuring out who is the **GOAT!**

Calculating trophies, honours and goals scored, we see who wins between the four players often regarded as the greatest – but there can be only one!

(Stats all taken from same source for consistency.)

POINTS KEY

- WORLD CUP WINNER = 10 POINTS
- EURO CHAMPIONSHIP WINNER = 8 POINTS
- COPA AMERICA WINNER = 8 POINTS
- CHAMPIONS LEAGUE WINNER = 6 POINTS
- COPA LIBERATORS = 6 POINTS
- PREMIER LEAGUE WINNER = 5 POINTS
- LA LIGA WINNER = 5 POINTS
- OTHER LEAGUE WINNER = 3 POINTS
- KNOCK-OUT CUPS = 2 POINTS
- GOALS SCORED = 1 POINT (PER GOAL)
- BALLON D'OR WINNER = 5 POINTS

Pele

World Cup winner x 3 = 30 pts
European Championship winner = (not eligible) 0
Copa America winner = 0
Champions League winner = 0
Copa Libertadores x 2 = 12 pts
Premier League winner = 0
La Liga winner = 0
Other domestic league winner x 6 = 18 pts
Knock-out cups (anywhere) x 19 = 38 pts
Goals scored in total career x 786 = 786 pts
Ballon d'Or winner x 8 = 40 pts

Total: 924 pts

Maradona

World Cup winner x 1 = 10 pts
European Championship winner = (not eligible)
Copa America winner = 0
Champions League winner = 0
Copa Liberators = 0
Premier League winner = 0
La Liga winner = 0
Other domestic league winner x 3 = 9 pts
Knock-out cups (anywhere) x 6 = 12 pts
Goals scored x 345 = 345 pts
Ballon d'Or winner = 0

Total: 376 pts

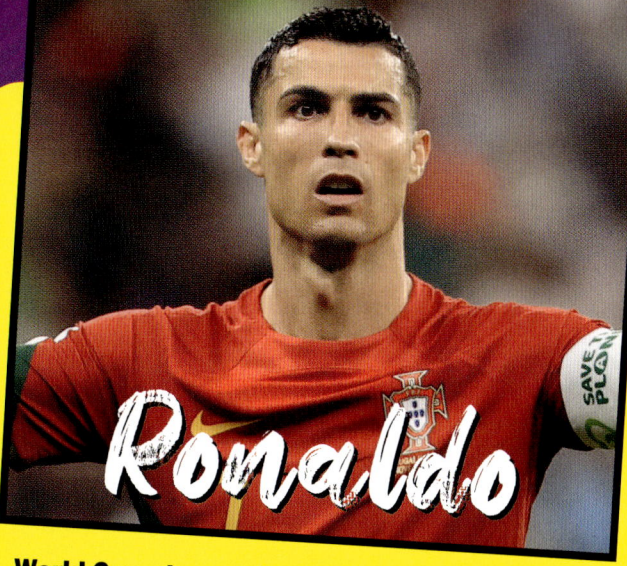

Ronaldo

World Cup winner = 0 pts
European Championship winner x 1 = 8 pts
Copa America winner = (not eligible)
Champions League winner x 5 = 30 pts
Copa Liberators = (not eligible)
Premier League winner x 3 = 15 pts
La Liga winner x 2 = 10 pts
Other domestic league winner x 2 = 6 pts
Knock-out cups (anywhere) x 18 = 36 pts
Goals scored x 885 = 885 pts
Ballon d'Or winner x 5 = 25 pts

Total: 1015 pts

Messi

World Cup winner x 1 = 10 pts
European Championship winner = (not eligible)
Copa America winner x 1 = 8 pts
Champions League winner x 4 = 24 pts
Copa Liberators = 0
Premier League winner = 0
La Liga winner x 10 = 50 pts
Other domestic league winner x 2 = 6 pts
Knock-out cups (anywhere) x 22 = 44 pts
Goals scored x 838 = 838 pts
Ballon d'Or winner x 8 = 40 pts

Total: 1020 pts

AND THE GOAT IS... Lionel Messi

But by just five points – and both Messi and second place Ronaldo are still playing, so *SHOOT* will revisit this when both players have retired...

SHOOT FOOTY QUIZ

So, you think you're a huge footy fan? Here is your chance to test your knowledge with this quick-fire quiz! Some questions are trickier than others, but everyone loves a challenge!

1. Player shirt number maths: Phil Foden's club shirt number + Declan Rice's club shirt number.

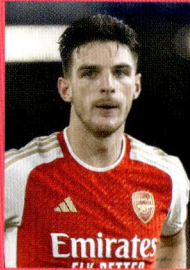

2. Can you name this Premier League Manager?

3. Which European league would you be playing in if you won this trophy?

4. Which EFL Championship team play their home games at this stadium?

5. Did Erling Haaland score more league goals in his first or second season for Manchester City?

6. Which national team did former Chelsea Women boss Emma Hayes become coach of in 2024?

7. Which former Everton, Fulham and Leicester winger scored a Europa League Final hat-trick?

8. Who is this Manchester City Women and Lionesses legend who retired in 2024?

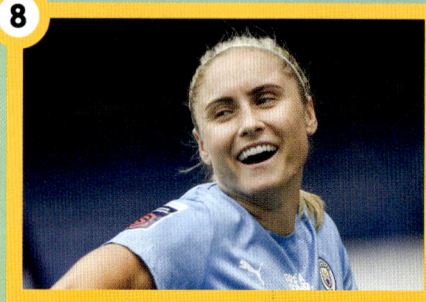

46

9 In total, how many club trophies has Harry Kane won so far? None, two or four?

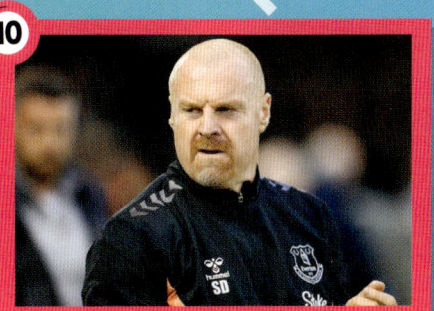

10 Which of these clubs has Sean Dyche NOT managed? Watford, Burnley or Southampton?

11 Alessia Russo joined Arsenal from which club in July 2023?

12 How many European Cups / Champions Leagues have Liverpool won?

13 Which of these English teams have NEVER played in the Premier League?

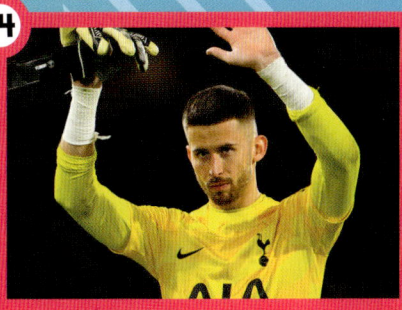

14 True or false? You can play a match without having a designated goalkeeper.

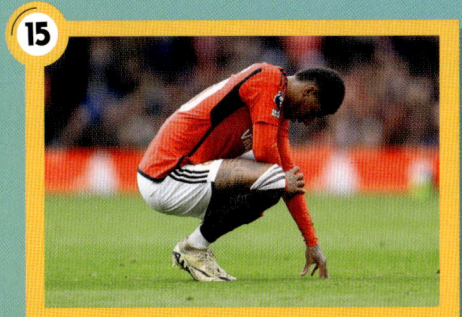

15 Manchester United hold the record for most FA Cup Final defeats. How many finals have they lost?

16 The 'Yellow Wall' is the nickname for the south stand at which German clubs' stadium?

17 Football pundit and Premier League record goalscorer Alan Shearer won the Premier League with which club?

18 Whose Premier League home game would you be at if you saw this mascot entertaining the crowd?

19 How many clean sheets did David Raya keep to claim the 2023/24 Golden Glove? 14, 16 or 18?

20 Which Dutch club did Arne Slot leave to become the new Liverpool manager?

ANSWERS ON PAGES 76-77

BEST

Sometimes, international kits are amazing – but sometimes they're just plain terrible! Here is *SHOOT*'s guide to the Top 5 best – and the Top 5 worst – see if you agree!

ENGLAND - 1966
An all-time classic – red shirts, white shorts, and a simple, effective design. Perfection!

ARGENTINA - 1986
A beautiful football shirt – Argentina's colour and design are unique in world football.

HOLLAND - 1974
Another all-time classic design – only the Dutch could get away with wearing an orange shirt!

BRAZIL - 1970
One of football's most iconic strips, these colours shouldn't work – but they look fantastic!

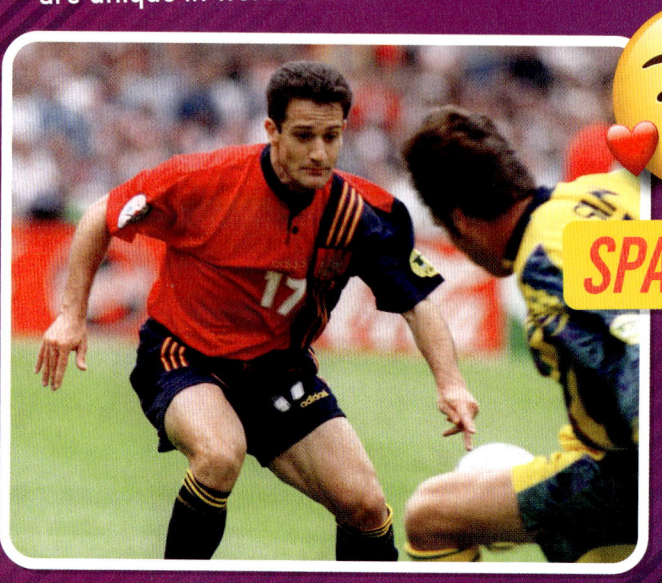

SPAIN - 1996
The Spanish kit always looks classy and strong – the 1996 variation was one of their best!

48

& WORST KITS... EVER!

NIGERIA - 1994
A mix between wearing newspapers and pyjamas – this was a bad design!

MEXICO - 1994
When the goalkeeper kit is so ugly it puts off the strikers, you know you're in trouble – ugh!

GERMANY - 1994
These colours just don't go together well and the design around the neck is just messy!

USA - 1994
Two words describe the US kit for 1994 – fashion disaster!

SCOTLAND - 1990
Yawn! A shirt that is beyond boring – how do these kits get approved?

FUTURE STAR
MORGAN ROGERS

SHOOT caught up for a Q&A with Aston Villa's exciting young winger, Morgan Rogers.

You joined in the January 2024 transfer window – how did it feel to join a club the size of Aston Villa?

"A bit surreal as I looked around the place for the first time, but it's an honour to be part of this team."

Why did you choose Villa?

"Obviously the size of the club, first and foremost, and the direction the club is going in is only positive and something I wanted to be part of. I used to play here as a kid. The facilities are amazing and have improved a lot since then!"

You're a local lad – are you happy to back in the Midlands?

"It's been a few years since I was back home, so it's nice to be back and around family and friends and playing locally again."

What are your aims as a player?

"I like to think I'm exciting to watch. I want to create chances and score goals, and I want to get fans out of their seats and play with a free spirit."

You can play a number of roles – what's your favourite position?

"I've always prided myself on the number of positions I can play; I've done that since I was young. I love the game and I know what each position entails. I have the football intelligence to know what's asked and to try to carry it out for the team. Some positions suit me more than others, of course, but I'm more than happy to play anywhere — as long as I'm on the pitch. That's the most important thing and always has been."

You and Jude Bellingham – another Midlands lad – are good friends and you call him 'little bro' on social media. How did that come about?

"We got to know each other and then he got picked for England in my age group — he was a year below — and we just got closer from there. We've been following each other since. I think everyone can see how well he's doing!"

AVFC

FACT FILE
- **CLUB:** Aston Villa
- **TURNED PRO:** 2019
- **COUNTRY:** England
- **POSITION:** Forward
- **BORN:** 26 July 2002

Cole Palmer is one of your best friends in football from your days at Man City – he's doing pretty well, too!

"Cole is one of the closest people I have in football and in life - someone I speak to consistently. When you see him doing so well it makes me happy and he's showing everyone now what I and others knew he could do two or three years ago and I'm so proud of him. It's a pleasure to see."

But he took your celebration, didn't he – the 'Cold Palmer' as it's known?

Yeah, he definitely copied it from me! Check the timeline – I did it first!"

You're a Premier League player now and have the Champions League to look forward to as well – it must be exciting for you?

"It's a dream come true for me, really – these are the competitions you want to play in and dream about when you're growing up. You want to compete against the best and I'm so grateful and honoured to be given the opportunity to be part of it and now it's down to me to show what I'm about and that I deserve to be here."

What are your personal targets?

"I'm still young, I know, but I want to be the best person I can be in my prime years. I back myself and believe in myself. Being an established Premier League player, I think everyone wants that."

51

FUTURE STAR

Q&A WITH LIVERPOOL AND NORTHERN IRELAND'S RISING TALENT...

You went on loan to Bolton Wanderers to begin with and were voted their 2022/23 Player of the Year.

"I'm so thankful to the staff and fans because I couldn't have dreamed I'd have such a wonderful year with Bolton – we won the EFL Trophy at Wembley and made the play-offs and I loved playing for Bolton because I had some incredible moments. I also improved as a person and a player. I'll always keep an eye on their results and hope they get back in the Championship as soon as possible."

Who was your idol as a kid?

"Gareth Bale was someone I watched quite a lot. He got his big move to Real Madrid and Wales are a small nation, but he did so well for Wales and was their best player for so many years. I was a winger as well, so he was someone I looked up to. He was an unbelievable player and some of the stuff on the pitch he did was magnificent."

You've already been compared by some to Gareth Bale - how does that feel?

"It's nice to get little comparisons like that, but I still think I have a long way to go to do what he's done. It's nice, but I'm still learning my trade."

How's your Premier League debut season been?

"It's been a whirlwind. A bit unreal, really."

CONOR BRADLEY

FACT FILE

CLUB: Liverpool
TURNED PRO: 2020
COUNTRY: Northern Ireland
POSITION: Full-back
BORN: 9 July 2003

When you've played, you have mostly filled in for Trent Alexander-Arnold – does that bring its own pressure?

"Yeah, obviously Trent is probably the best right-back in the world at the moment, if not the best player in the world the way he's playing. Obviously I'm not Trent Alexander-Arnold, so I'm just going to play my game and just contribute what I can to the team. Hopefully that does us well."

What would you say to young players who are being versatile in the modern game?

"It is massive to be versatile. At Liverpool we have Trent Alexander-Arnold. He is an unbelievable footballer and I think he could play pretty much anywhere. There are so many things I can take from him. It helps the manager to pick you when he knows you can play in certain positions. I am pretty versatile myself. I played as a winger all the way up through youth football and I was deployed to play there the other night for Northern Ireland and really enjoyed it. I enjoy the challenge of playing new positions and learning about them."

Your Liverpool debut saw you win 4-0 at Bournemouth – and claim an assist – how did that feel?

"I don't think I could put it into words, really. It was so special and something I'd wanted and been dreaming about for a long time, so to play and get an assist as well was fantastic."

In only your second Premier League appearance, you scored one and assisted two more in a 4-1 win over Chelsea - how was that?

"It was probably that game where I thought, 'Right, I can do this'. I just need to be consistent with it and try to do things like that as much as I can. It's obviously difficult coming into one of the best teams in the world and trying to break through and prove that you're good enough to play every week. That was a big moment for me where I realised that this is possible. My friends were over for the game, so they were back at my apartment after and I just remember saying to them, 'What's just happened?' It was crazy! It was just mental the whole couple days later. I just couldn't believe what was happening to be honest with you."

You won the Premier League Fans' Player of the Month, scored a goal, got several assists and then won the Carabao Cup – all in the space of a few weeks – did you pinch yourself that it was all happening?

"A bit! I couldn't have dreamed it would have gone quite as well as it has and now I just have to keep it going, keep working hard and try to improve myself because I know there's a lot of improvement I can make."

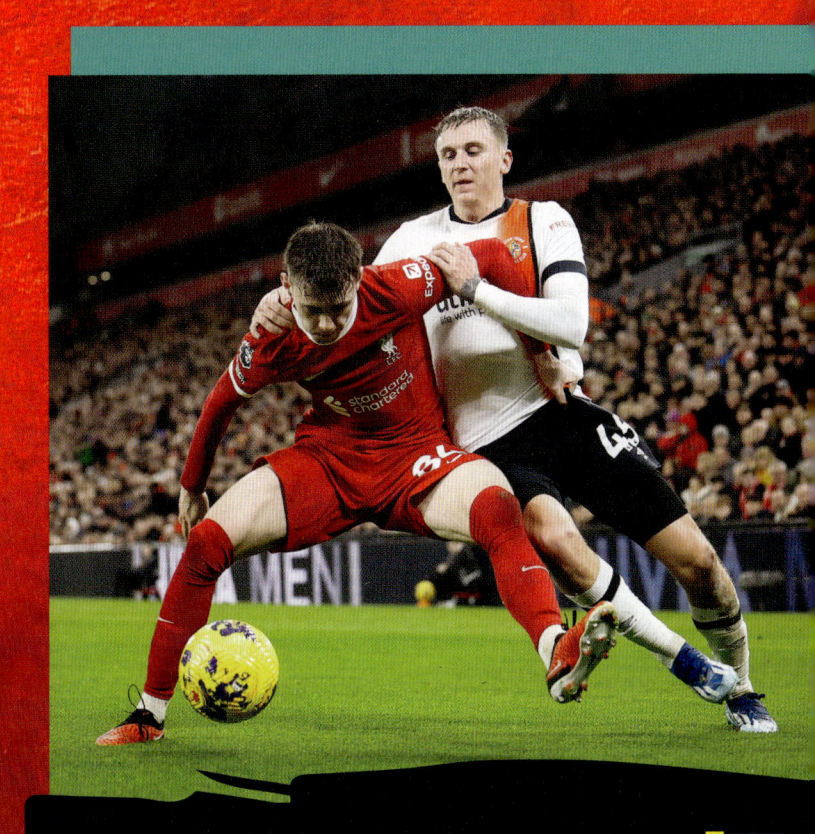

53

SPOT THE DIFFERENCE

Look closely at Picture A and Picture B – they're the same, right? Wrong! There are TEN differences in Picture B – the question is, can you spot them all? Circle the ones you find.

A

B

1
2
3
4
5
6
7
8
9
10

ANSWERS ON PAGES 76-77

54

LEON BAILEY

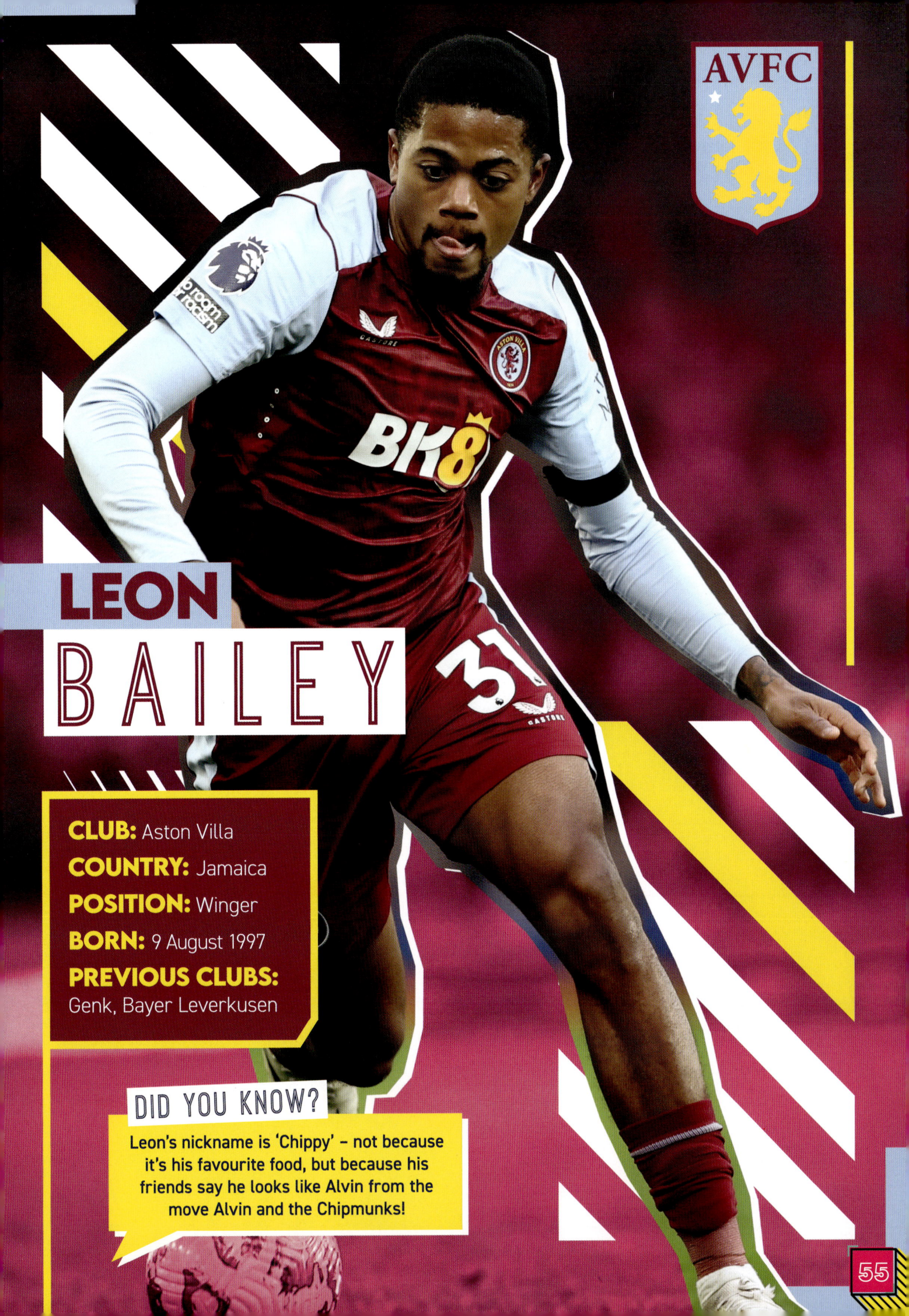

CLUB: Aston Villa
COUNTRY: Jamaica
POSITION: Winger
BORN: 9 August 1997
PREVIOUS CLUBS: Genk, Bayer Leverkusen

DID YOU KNOW?

Leon's nickname is 'Chippy' – not because it's his favourite food, but because his friends say he looks like Alvin from the move Alvin and the Chipmunks!

SCANDINAVIAN DREAM TEAM

Scandinavian football is on the crest of a wave – and to prove it, *SHOOT* looks at the very best talent from Norway, Denmark, and Sweden…

Premier League's Top Six Scandic Talents!

ERLING HAALAND
NORWAY + MAN CITY

The prolific Norwegian has been a smash hit in the Premier League and has won the Golden Boot in his first two seasons with Manchester City. An icon in his homeland and a superstar around the world – what a talent!

ALEXANDER ISAK
SWEDEN + NEWCASTLE

Injuries and inconsistency meant Alexander Isak's first season with Newcastle United was decent but not spectacular – his second campaign, however, has shown what a talent he is with the elegant Swede now considered one of the best strikers in the Premier League – and Europe.

MARTIN ODEGAARD
NORWAY + ARSENAL

After dazzling as a teenager, Martin Odegaard's star faded for several years after joining Real Madrid – but since joining Arsenal he's become the heart and soul of Mikel Arteta's exciting team. In many ways, he is the complete midfielder.

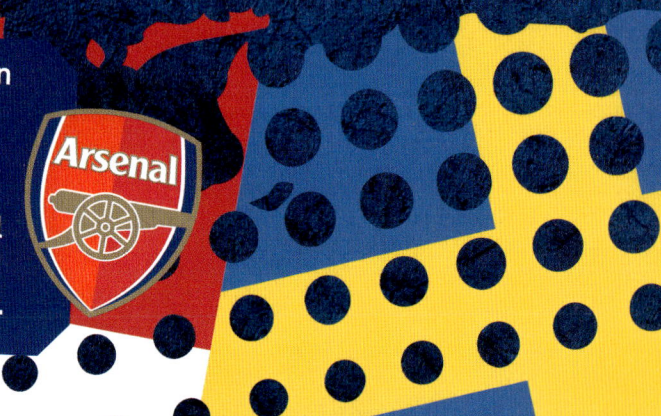

DEJAN KULUSEVSKI
SWEDEN + SPURS

A versatile player, Dejan Kulusevski has become one of the main components of Ange Postecoglou's Tottenham team. A dangerous wide man, his crosses and ability to chip in with important goals make him another top Scandinavian.

KRISTOFFER AJER
NORWAY + BRENTFORD

A huge talent in every sense! The former Celtic centre-back stands at six feet, six inches tall and is a man-mountain of a defender. He's become a vital member of Brentford's team and a highly respected Premier League player.

OSCAR BOBB
NORWAY + MAN CITY

The dazzling City winger made a huge impression during his breakthrough season at the Etihad. Blessed with mesmerising skills and electric pace, no wonder Pep Guardiola has tied him down to a long contract!

PL NORDIC LEGENDS

Here are five players from the past who lit up the Premier League...

FREDDIE LJUNGBERG
SWEDEN

PETER SCHMEICHEL
DENMARK

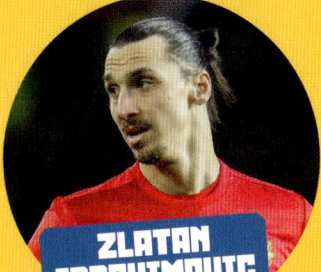

ZLATAN IBRAHIMOVIC
SWEDEN

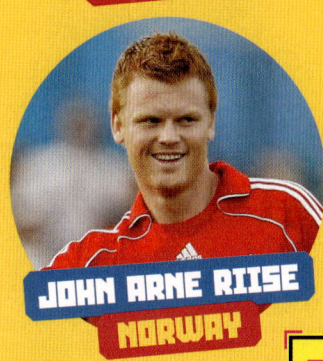

OLE GUNNAR SOLSKJAER
NORWAY

JOHN ARNE RIISE
NORWAY

2024 WINNERS

This year has seen loads of awesome champions crowned. Take a look back at the winners from around the world, plus you can fill in the blanks. It's trophy time!

DOMESTIC

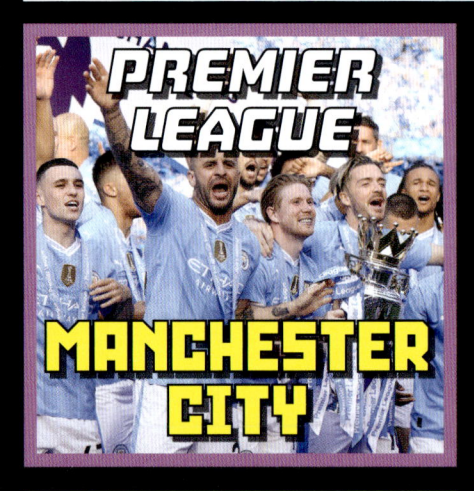

PREMIER LEAGUE
MANCHESTER CITY

FA CUP
MANCHESTER UNITED

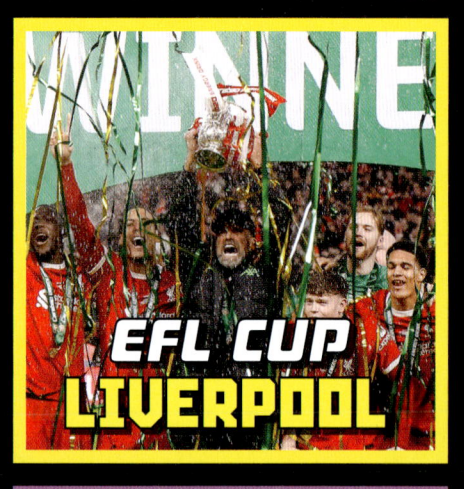

EFL CUP
LIVERPOOL

CHAMPIONSHIP
LEICESTER CITY

Promoted
Ipswich Town, Southampton (play-offs)

LEAGUE ONE
PORTSMOUTH

Promoted
Derby County, Oxford United (play-offs)

LEAGUE TWO
STOCKPORT

Promoted
Wrexham, Mansfield Town, Crewe Alexandra (play-offs)

NATIONAL LEAGUE
1st: Chesterfield
Promoted: Bromley

SCOTTISH PREMIERSHIP
Celtic

SCOTTISH CUP
Celtic

SCOTTISH LEAGUE CUP
Rangers

NIFL PREMIERSHIP
Larn

CYMRU PREMIER
The New Saints

COMMUNITY SHIELD

58

EUROPE

LA LIGA (Spain)
1st: Real Madrid
2nd: Barcelona

BUNDESLIGA (Germany)
1st: Bayer Leverkusen
2nd: Bayern Munich

LIGUE 1 (France)
1st: Paris Saint-Germain
2nd: Monaco

SERIE A (Italy)
1st: Inter
2nd: AC Milan

EREDIVISIE (Netherlands)
1st: PSV Eindhoven
2nd: Feyenoord

PRIMEIRA LIGA (Portugal)
1st: Sporting
2nd: Benfica

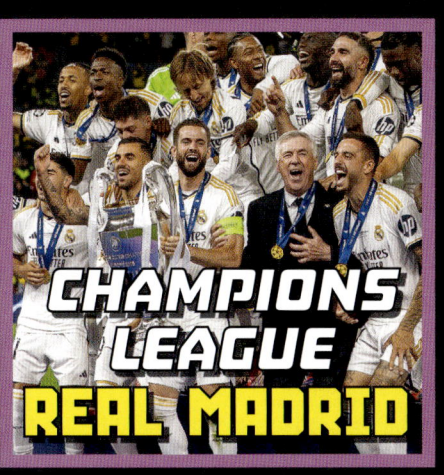

CHAMPIONS LEAGUE
REAL MADRID

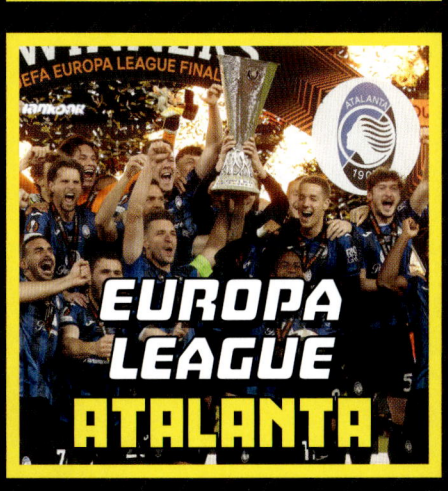

EUROPA LEAGUE
ATALANTA

EUROPA CONFERENCE
OLYMPIACOS

WOMEN

WSL
CHELSEA

FA CUP
MANCHESTER UNITED

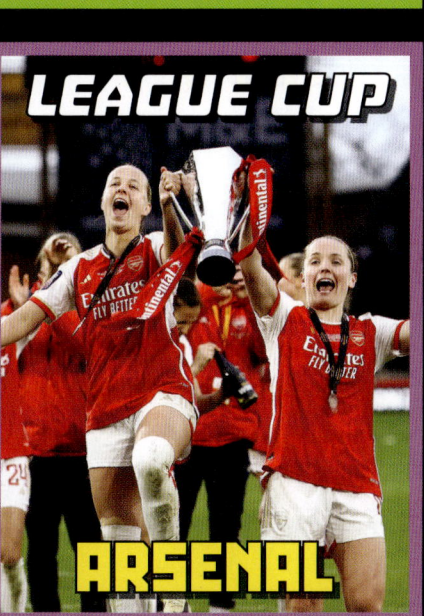

UEFA SUPER CUP

INTERNATIONAL

UEFA EURO'S (MENS)

LEAGUE CUP
ARSENAL

CHAMPIONS LEAGUE
BARCELONA

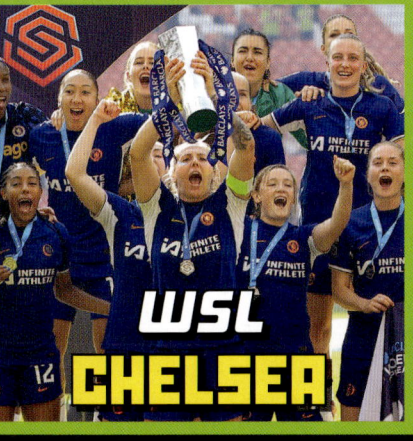

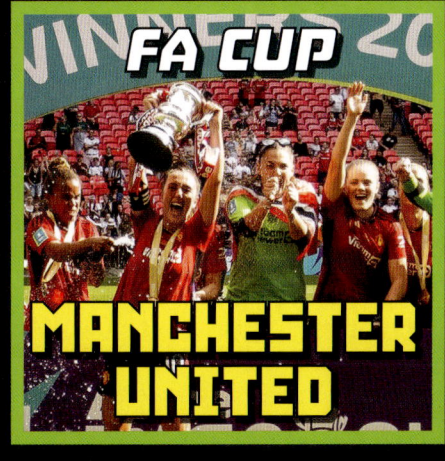

CHAMPIONSHIP
1st: Crystal Palace

PHIL FODEN
TROPHY HUNTER

For a player who is still only 24, **PHIL FODEN** has won more trophies than most players will win in a lifetime! The Manchester City and England playmaker could become one of the most decorated footballers of all time if he continues the way he has been – here is a break down of his incredible silverware haul so far...

1 x UEFA CHAMPIONS LEAGUE

Having been a runner-up in 2021, Phil won his first Champions League in 2023 as City beat Inter 1-0 in Istanbul. He came off the bench on 36 minutes to replace the injured Kevin De Bruyne and gave a top performance for the Blues on an historic night for the club.

5 x PREMIER LEAGUES

Phil has notched up five Premier League titles so far – in just seven years! His influence on a fantastic Manchester City team just seems to get better each year with 2023-24 his best yet in terms of appearances and goals.

2 x FA CUPS

Foden has two FA Cup winners medals including the 2-1 win over Manchester United in the 2023 final.

4 x LEAGUE CUPS

The EFL Cup – or Carabao Cup – was a trophy City enjoyed winning up until 2021, having won it four years in a row since 2017. That's four more winner's medals for Phil!

2 x FA COMMUNITY SHIELD

The annual English curtain raiser, usually played between the winner of the Premier League and the FA Cup, has been won twice by the player City fans call the 'Stockport Iniesta'

1 x UEFA SUPER CUP

City, as defending champions of Europe, took on Europa League winners Sevilla and after the game ended 1-1, the Blues won 5-4 on penalties.

1 x FIFA CLUB WORLD CUP

City earned the right to be called champions of the world with their first FIFA Club World Cup triumph in Saudi Arabia. Phil was one of the scorers in the 4-0 final win over Brazilian side Fluminense.

1 x FIFA U-17 WORLD CUP

Foden scored twice in the 5-2 win over Spain as England won the Under-17 World Cup – and he won the coveted 'Golden Ball' award after being voted the most valuable player of the tournament.

INDIVIDUAL AWARDS

Just for good measure, here's some of the top individual awards he's won! What a player!

UEFA European Under-17 Championship Team of the Tournament: 2017

FIFA U-17 World Cup Golden Ball: 2017

BBC Young Sports Personality of the Year: 2017

UEFA Champions League Squad of the Season: 2020–21

Premier League Young Player of the Season: 2020–21, 2021–22

PFA Young Player of the Year: 2020–21, 2021–22

BARCLAYS WOMEN'S SUPER LEAGUE

TOP STATS!

It was an exciting season for women's football yet again with so many out of this world performances, a title race decided on goal-difference, and a farewell to some WSL legends. Here is *SHOOT's* WSL supercharged rundown of the 2023/24 season!

HONOURS BOARD

Champions: Chelsea
Runners-up: Manchester City
Promoted to the WSL: Crystal Palace
FA Women's Cup: Manchester United
Continental Cup: Arsenal
WSL Player of the Season: Khadija Shaw (Man City)
WSL Manager of the Season: Matt Beard (Liverpool)

MOST GOALS SCORED (TEAM)

Chelsea 71 goals
Manchester City 61 goals
Arsenal 53 goals
Manchester United 42 goals
Liverpool 36 goals

MOST GOALS CONCEDED (TEAM)

Bristol City 70 goals
Brighton 48 goals
Leicester City 45 goals
West Ham United 45 goals
Aston Villa 43 goals

MOST GOALS SCORED (PLAYER)

Khadija Shaw (Man City) 20 goals
Lauren James (Chelsea) 13 goals
Elisabeth Terland (Brighton) 13 goals
Alessia Russo (Arsenal) 12 goals

MOST ASSISTS

Lauren Hemp (Man City) 8 assists
Mary Fowler (Man City)
Johanna Rytting-Kaneryd (Chesea)
Niamh Charles (Chelsea)
Katie Zelem (Man United)
6 assists

TOP 5 CROWDS

60,160 Arsenal v Man United
60,050 Arsenal v Spurs
59,042 Arsenal v Chelsea
54,115 Arsenal v Liverpool
43,615 Man United v Man City

CLEAN SHEETS

Khiara Keating (Man City) 9 clean sheets
Mary Earps (Man United) 7 clean sheets
Hannah Hampton (Chelsea) 6 clean sheets
Rachael Laws (Liverpool)
Manuela Zinsberger (Arsenal)
Courtney Brosnan (Everton)
5 clean sheets

Players and their Pets

Top footballers love their pets just as much as they love football, so we've found a selection of players who are proud to show off their beloved furry friends...

BERNARDO SILVA
The Portugal star with his two dogs, John and Charles!
Credit: @bernardocarvalhosilva

MO SALAH
Many say Mo is the purrfect striker, so no wonder he adores cats.
Credit: @mosalah

THOMAS MULLER
The Germany star has a love of horses – here he is with his wife and Dave!
Credit: @esmuellert

KAI HAVERTZ
Arsenal's forward has a lifelong love of donkeys – and now has his own collection!
Credit: @kaihavertz29

LIONEL MESSI
I think we all agree that Leo's dog Hulk is incredible, but do you think the GOAT owns a goat? Now that would be funny!
Credit: @leomessi

CHLOE KELLY
Lionesses star Chloe Kelly chills out with her two pooches.
Credit: @chloekelly

JAMES MILNER
Milner's love of dogs is well-known – one of them is photobombing this picture!
Credit: @jamesmilnerofficial

ANIMAL SPOTTING

Continuing our animal theme, these club badges should all feature an animal but they've gone missing! Can you match the right animal with the right badge? Good luck!

Aston Villa | **Atletico Madrid** | **Coventry** | **Valencia**

Ipswich Town | **Roma** | **Watford** | **Benfica**

Bat 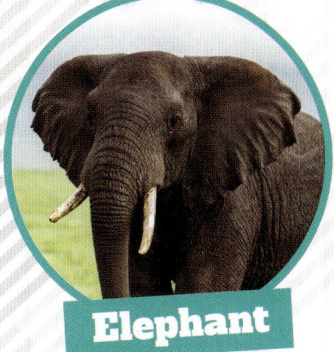 | **Elephant**  | **Horse**  | **Bear**

Wolf  | **Eagle**  | **Moose**  | **Lion**

ANSWERS ON PAGES 76-77

DECLAN RICE 10 FACTS

10 Declan spent seven years with Chelsea's academy - but was released and joined West Ham instead.

9 His favourite pre-match meal - no matter when the kick-off time is - is sea bass and rice.

8 His hobbies outside of football include golf, darts, pool, walking his dogs and collecting sneakers!

7 Though he chose Arsenal over Manchester City, Declan has three framed shirts of City players in his pool room - David Silva, Kevin De Bruyne and Sergio Aguero.

6 His footballing idols are Sergio Busquets, Ngolo Kante and Yaya Toure.

5 Two of his closest friends in football were both with him at Chelsea's academy - Mason Mount and Eddie Nketiah.

4 His first senior goal was scored against... Arsenal!

3 While with West Ham, Rice won three Young Player of the Season awards and another three as Player of the Season.

2 He may have won more than 50 caps for England, but he started out playing for Republic of Ireland where he won three senior caps before switching allegiances.

1 He wears the No.41 shirt for the Gunners as that was his first senior squad number at West Ham - and it's served him pretty well so far!

MICKY VAN DE VEN

CLUB: Tottenham Hotspur
COUNTRY: Netherlands
POSITION: Defender
BORN: 19 April 2001
PREVIOUS CLUBS: Volendam, VfL Wolfsburg

DID YOU KNOW?

Mickey Van de Ven became the fastest recorded Premier League player when he clocked an incredible 23.23 miles per hour in January 2024!

DID YOU

Here's a bunch of facts and crazy football stats to impress your friends with – unless they own a copy of the SHOOT 2025 Annual, of course!

BURUNDI DE BRUYNE?

Manchester City's **Kevin De Bruyne** has been one of Belgium's best players, but did you know he could have been Burundi's greatest ever player? Kevin's mum was born in Burundi, who are ranked 140 in the world – so KDB could have represented them instead if he had wanted.

I'M NOT CHANTING THAT!

Imagine trying to sing a song with the world's longest football club name in it? Well, Dutch Eredivisie side NAC Breda could have had that problem if the club hadn't shortened their name! Their full title is: **Nooit opgeven altijd doorzetten, Aangenaam door vermaaken nuttig door ontspanning, Combinatie Breda** - those words mean: Never give up, always persevere, pleasant for its entertainment and useful for its relaxation. What a name!

PLAY UP POMPEY!

Imagining having the FA Cup for seven seasons as champions? That's seven wins at Wembley in the final, right? Wrong! **Portsmouth** hold the record for the having the FA Cup for a record seven years, but after they won the trophy in 1939, professional football was suspended for seven years due to World War 2. So, even though Pompey won it in 1939, they could still claim to be defending champions by 1946!

SANCHOOOOO!

Jadon Sancho holds the unique record of being the first player born in the 21st century (2000-onwards) to play for England when he made his debut for the Three Lions against Croatia in October 2018.

KNOW?

HOW OLD?

Which is the oldest club in England? Aston Villa? Arsenal? Maybe Newcastle United? The answer is Sheffield – not Sheffield United or Wednesday – but **Sheffield FC** who were founded in 1857! Today, they play their games at - fittingly - Home of Football Ground, which has a capacity of 2,089.

KIWI POWER!

Who were the only unbeaten side at the 2010 World Cup? Winners Spain, surely? No! It was - wait for it - **New Zealand**. Yep, the Kiwis drew all three of their group stage games. Eventual winners Spain - who scored only eight goals in total during the tournament - lost their opening game to Switzerland.

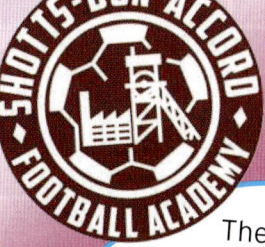

IS IT OVER YET, REF?

The poor players of **Bon Accord** forever etched their name into the history books in September 1885. Playing away to Arbroath in the Scottish Cup, Bon Accord managed to lose 36-0! Of course, their fans believe that had there been two legs, they could probably have turned the tie around!

KINGS OF SPAIN!

Real Madrid, Barcelona, Atletico Madrid, Valencia, Athletic Bilboa and Sevila have all won the Copa del Rey... and **Motherwell**! That's right, in 1927, both Motherwell and Swansea were invited to take part in the Spanish cup competition, with Motherwell beating Real Madrid 3-1 in the final!

LUCKY XAVI

Some would say being a professional footballer is a lucky profession to have – of course, they are lucky to have been born with such skills, but plenty of hard work and dedication has also gone into their career. But Barcelona legend **Xavi** really is lucky - in 2017, he won the Qatari national lottery of one million riyals - about £210,000!

69

EXCLUSIVE
COLE PALMER

After an impressive first season with the Blues, *SHOOT* met with one of the most exciting players in the Premier League....

What are your earliest memories of football?

"Going with my dad to the local park, which was about two minutes away from where I used to live in Manchester. Without my dad, I don't think I would be a professional footballer today."

As a Manchester lad, is it true you were a Manchester United fan as a kid?

"Yes, when I was growing up, I was a Manchester United fan."

Your unique style is both exciting and original - do you think a lot before the ball comes to you?

"I try and think a bit about what I will do, but mostly it's just natural to me and I don't think too much in advance."

Your penalty technique has paid off so far - what exactly is your penalty thinking?

"I honestly don't even have one! I just put the ball down on the spot, step back and shoot! A couple of times I changed my mind as I ran up. I did miss one in the FA Youth Cup final with City against Liverpool. I was gutted because we should have won."

Where does the nickname 'Cold' come from?

"I saw all the comments on my social media saying 'cold, cold, cold' so I thought I'd do it as a celebration."

Is it true you got the celebration from your former Man City Academy team-mate (now at Villa), Morgan Rogers?

"Yeah - but he understands - it didn't make sense for him to do it!"

70

Have you enjoyed living in London after leaving City?

"I'm getting used to it. It was a big change because I'd never played for another club, or even been out on loan anywhere, and I moved away from my family in Manchester for the first time, but I just thought, 'I'll give it a go'."

FACT FILE

CLUB: Chelsea
TURNED PRO: 2020
COUNTRY: England
POSITION: Winger, Attacking midfielder
BORN: 6 May 2002

Your first season as a Chelsea player couldn't have gone much better - did you surprise yourself?

"Of course - I didn't think things would happen this quickly - maybe eventually - but not this fast, but this was my first season playing all the time. I'm kind of getting used to it. I just try and get on the ball and try and make things happen."

Did Mauricio Pochettino improve you as a player?

"He's improved me a lot and given me the licence to get on the ball wherever the team needs me to be and that's what I love to do - play with freedom and do my stuff."

SILLY SHADOWS

Everyone loves a silly club mascot! We have put six mascots in silhouettes to see if you can figure out who they are and what club they belong to – we've added a few clues to help!

A
- I live in North London.
- I'm millions of years old!
- NAME:
- CLUB:

B
- You can find me in a toolbox!
- I'm 100% iron!
- NAME:
- CLUB:

C
- I come from outer space!
- I love the sky to be blue.
- NAME:
- CLUB:

NAMES
HAMMERHEAD MIGHTY RED GUNNERSAURUS FRED THE RED MOONCHESTER BELLA

CLUBS
ASTON VILLA MANCHESTER CITY LIVERPOOL WEST HAM UNITED ARSENAL MANCHESTER UNITED

D
- I'm a cheeky red devil!
- I love OT, and I don't mean overtime!
- NAME:
- CLUB:

E
- I'm a bit of a villain.
- I love to roar in the park!
- NAME:
- CLUB:

F
- I never walk alone!
- I can fly over the Kop!
- NAME:
- CLUB:

ANSWERS ON PAGES 76-77

TRANSFER CHALLENGE

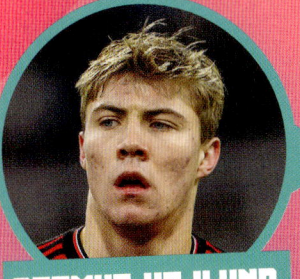

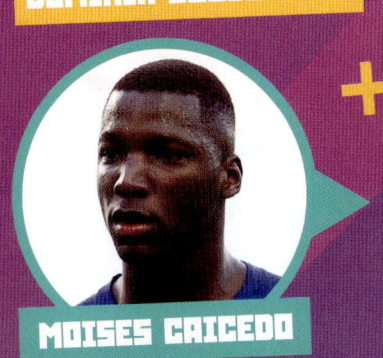

Here's a test of your transfer knowledge. Can you connect the player to the transfer amount they cost and the two clubs involved? It's a mega money match-up! To kick things off, we've done the first one for you. You're welcome!

PLAYER	TRANSFER FEE	FROM	TO
Rasmus Hojlund	£60 million	BVB 09	Liverpool
Jude Bellingham	£115 million	Brighton & Hove Albion	Manchester United
Jordan Henderson	£64 million	Ettifaq Club	Chelsea
Dominik Szoboszlai	FREE TRANSFER	Atalanta 1907	Real Madrid
Moises Caicedo	£88 million	RB Leipzig	Ajax Amsterdam

ANSWERS ON PAGES 76-77

73

JUDE BELLINGHAM

From Birmingham to the Berbabeu, *SHOOT* takes a look at the journey of the games newest Galactico...

Born in Stourbridge near Birmingham, Jude Bellingham's journey to becoming one of the best young footballers in the world began when he started to shine in schoolboy football.

His dad Mark was a police officer who also played at non-League level where he scored plenty of goals – maybe his dad could have made it if he'd not had a career in the police to focus on?

Perhaps that's why he spent so much time playing football with his oldest son as well as his younger son, Jobe.

Jude was soon playing for Stourbridge FC and, as a keen Birmingham City fan, joined Blues' Under-8 team and was soon attracting interest as a player of huge promise.

74

By the age of 14, he was already playing for Birmingham's Under-18 team! By 15, Jude had made his debut for the Under-23 side and scouts from some of Europe's top clubs were really starting to take notice.

He was training with the senior team and it was only a matter of time before he made his first team debut having been given the No.22 shirt for the 2019/20 season. On August 6, 2019, Bellingham became Blues' youngest ever debutant, aged 16 years and 38 days, in a League Cup tie against Portsmouth.

He would go on to play 44 games that season, scoring four goals and becoming a huge fan favourite in the process. Clubs were soon queuing up to buy him and though a £20m bid from Manchester United was rejected, a £25m bid from Borussia Dortmund was accepted, and at 17, he became the world's most expensive player of his age.

At Dortmund, Bellingham just kept getting better, playing in a side challenging for the Bundesliga title and domestic trophies, and playing Champions League football on a regular basis.

In November 2020, things got even better for Jude when he was called up for his England debut against Republic of Ireland. He remained in Germany for three full seasons, playing 124 times and scoring 24 goals. Such was his form, that during the summer of 2023, the world's top clubs were desperate to add the 20-year-old to their squad.

Manchester City, Liverpool and PSG were all said to have offered close to £100m for Bellingham, but when Real Madrid's offer was discussed, he accepted the chance to play for Los Blancos and become a legendary Galactico.

He would later say moving to the Bernabeu was a "no brainer" because of the club's history and standing. By the end of his first season in Madrid, he had added goals and numerous assists to his game, as the Spanish giants won La Liga and chased Champions League glory with victory against Dortmund.

Now an integral member of the England side, he is one of English football's brightest talents – and is likely to get better and better.

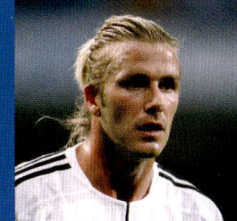

OTHER ENGLISH PLAYERS WHO HAVE PLAYED FOR REAL MADRID

MICHAEL OWEN
(2004-05)

DAVID BECKHAM
(2003-07)

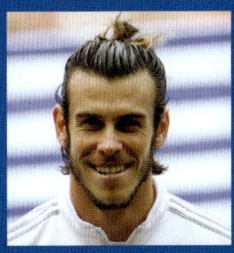

GARETH BALE
(2013-22)

STEVE McMANAMAN
(1999-2003)

CAROLINE WEIR
(2022-PRESENT)

JONATHAN WOODGATE
(2004-07)

LAURIE CUNNINGHAM
(1979-84)

ANSWERS

08 3 IN A ROW

Phil Foden - 47 - Man City.
Jarrod Bowen - 20 - West Ham.
Beth Mead - 9 - Arsenal.
Alexis Mac Allister - 10 - Liverpool.
Alex Iwobi - 22 - Fulham.
Micky van de Ven - 37 - Spurs.
Sam Kerr - 20 - Chelsea.
Ollie Watkins - 11 - Aston Villa.
Bruno Fernandes - 8 - Man United.
Alexander Isak - 14 - Newcastle.

09 CHAMPIONSHP CHALLENGE

10 CROWD CONTROL

Old Trafford - 74,310.
Nou Camp - 105,000.
Anfield - 61,015.
Parc Des Prince - 47,929.
Allianz Arena - 75,024.
Celtic Park - 60,411.
St James' Park - 52,404.

14-15 SPOT THE BALL

GAME 1: Ball C.
GAME 2: Ball F.
GAME 3: Ball D.
GAME 4: Ball B.

16-17 RULES OF THE GAME

Yellow & red cards - 1970.
VAR - 2019.
3 points for a win - 1981.
Goal-line technology - 2014.
The back-pass rule - 1992.
Penalty shoot-outs - 1970.

EXTRA TIME

1: True.
2: True.
3: False, the opposition is awarded the win by the referee.
4: True.
5: False, it must take a touch before going in the goal.
6: True.

22-23 SPOT THE BOSS

24-25 SHOOTS A-Z QUIZ

A: Aston Villa.
B: Blades.
C: City.
D: Defender.
E: Everton.
F: France.
G: Gunners.
H: Hat-trick.
I: Iraola.
J: Jarrod.
K: Kulusevski.
L: Leah.
M: Miss.
N: Netherlands.
O: Old Trafford.
P: Penalty.
Q: QPR.
R: Robertson.
S: Shoot.
T: Toney.
U: United.
V: Van De Ven.
W: Wolves.
X: Xhaka.
Y: Yellow.
Z: Zaha.

34 BADGE MASH-UP!

BADGE 1
Premier League: Chelsea.
Bundesliga: Borrusia Dortmund.
La Liga: Real Madrid.
Serie A: Inter Milan.

BADGE 2
Premier League: West Ham.
Bundesliga: Wolfsburg.
La Liga: Valencia.
Serie A: Roma.

BADGE 3
Premier League: Crystal Palace.
Bundesliga: Bayern Munich.
La Liga: Barcelona.
Serie A: Napoli.

BADGE 4
Premier League: Wolves.
Bundesliga: Bayer Leverkusen.
La Liga: Real Sociedad.
Serie A: AC Milan.

35 TRUE OR FALSE

1: False.
2: True.
3: True.
4: True.
5: True.
6: False.
7: False.
8: False.
9: False.
10: True.
11: True.
12: True.

46-47 SHOOT FOOTY QUIZ

1: 47 + 41 = 88.
2: Kieran McKenna.
3: German Bundesliga.
4: Sunderland.
5: First.
6: USA.
7: Ademola Lookman.
8: Steph Houghton.
9: None.
10: Southampton.
11: Manchester United.
12: Six.
13: Preston North End.
14: False.
15: Nine.
16: Borussia Dortmund.
17: Blackburn Rovers.
18: Brighton.
19: 16.
20: Feyenoord.

54 SPOT THE DIFFERENCE

65 ANIMAL SPOTTING

Aston Villa - Lion.
Atletico Madrid - Bear.
Coventry - Elephant.
Valencia - Bat.
Ipswich Town - Horse.
Roma - Wolf.
Watford - Moose.
Benfica - Eagle.

72 SILLY SHADOWS

A: Gunnersaurus - Arsenal.
B: Hammerhead - West Ham United.
C: Moonchester - Manchester City.
D: Fred the Red - Manchester United.
E: Bella - Aston Villa.
F: Mighty Red - Liverpool.

73 TRANSFER CHALLENGE

Rasmus Hojlund > £64m > Atalanta > Manchester United.
Jude Bellingham > £88m > Borussia Dortmund > Real Madrid.
Jordan Henderson > FREE > Al-Ettifaq > Ajax.
Dominik Szoboszlai > £60 > RB Leipzig > Liverpool.
Moises Caicedo > £115 > Brighton > Chelsea.

VISIT SHOOT.CO.UK
NOW THE VOICE OF FOOTBALL ONLINE

For the latest football news, interviews, transfer gossip, stats and much more.

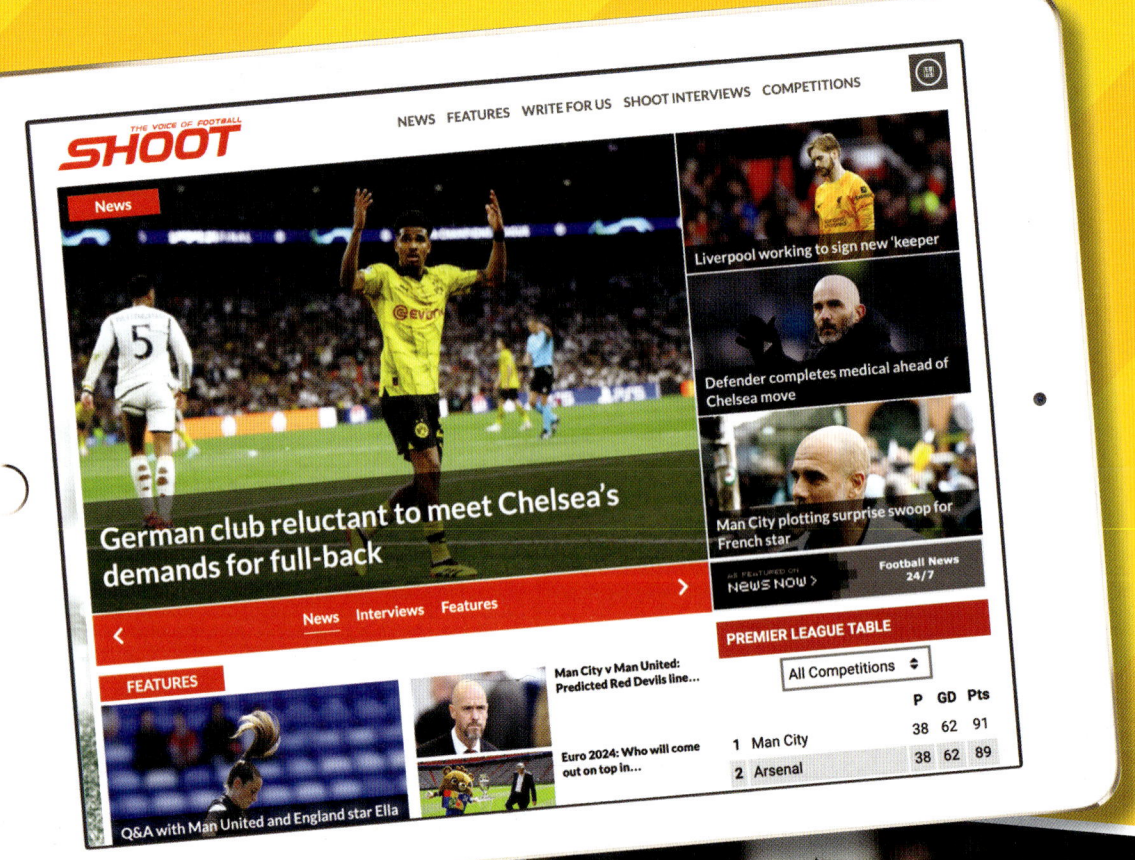

OVER 1.2 MILLION
UNIQUE PAGE VIEWS PER YEAR!

(Information/figures correct as of: July 2024)